"It's just us here." The words slipped out of her, impetuous, desperate.

A distant part of Eden urged her to show some sense. She knew Micah would never forgive her for so much as getting in Remy's car, but they had had something in Paris. It had been interrupted, and the not knowing what could have been had left her with an ache of yearning that had stalled her in some way. If she couldn't have Remy, then it didn't matter who she married. They were all the same because they weren't him.

"No one would know."

"This would only be today. An hour. We can't tell anyone. Ever. If Hunter found out..."

"If Micah found out..." she echoed with a catch in her voice. "I don't care about any of that, Remy. I really don't."

"After this, it goes back to the way it was, like we didn't even know one another. Is that really what you want?" His face twisted with conflict.

"No," she confessed with a chasm opening in her chest. "But I'll take it."

He closed his eyes, swearing as he fell back against the door with a defeated thump.

"Come here, then."

Four Weddings and a Baby

You are cordially invited to...the scandal of the wedding season!

In a shocking turn of events, the marriage of billionaire Hunter Waverly, aka the groom, was halted today when it was revealed he has a secret baby with a local waitress! Their one night clearly wasn't enough...but will this be a real-life Cinderella story?

And the drama doesn't stop there. Our sources say humiliated bride Eden decided to take matters—or should we say, the diamond ring—into her own hands and eloped with best man Remy Sylvain! Well, those two have always had a special connection since that night in Paris...

Meanwhile, maid of honor Quinn is rumored to have been whisked away by Eden's brother Micah. And the groom's sister Vienna? Let's just say she has the biggest secret of all...

It's never a dull moment at a billion-dollar society wedding!

Don't miss Hunter and Amelia's story in
Cinderella's Secret Baby

Read Remy and Eden's story in
Wedding Night with the Wrong Billionaire

Both available now!

And look out for
Micah and Quinn's story
and
Vienna and Jasper's story

Coming soon!

Dani Collins

WEDDING NIGHT WITH THE WRONG BILLIONAIRE

HARLEQUIN
PRESENTS

Recycling programs
for this product may
not exist in your area.

ISBN-13: 978-1-335-58400-7

Wedding Night with the Wrong Billionaire

Copyright © 2022 by Dani Collins

All rights reserved. No part of this book may be used or reproduced in
any manner whatsoever without written permission except in the case of
brief quotations embodied in critical articles and reviews.

This is a work of fiction. Names, characters, places and incidents
are either the product of the author's imagination or are used fictitiously.
Any resemblance to actual persons, living or dead, businesses,
companies, events or locales is entirely coincidental.

For questions and comments about the quality of this book,
please contact us at CustomerService@Harlequin.com.

Harlequin Enterprises ULC
22 Adelaide St. West, 41st Floor
Toronto, Ontario M5H 4E3, Canada
www.Harlequin.com

Printed in U.S.A.

Canadian **Dani Collins** knew in high school that she wanted to write romance for a living. Twenty-five years later, after marrying her high school sweetheart, having two kids with him, working at several generic office jobs and submitting countless manuscripts, she got The Call. Her first Harlequin novel won the Reviewers' Choice Award for Best First in Series from *RT Book Reviews*. She now works in her own office, writing romance.

Books by Dani Collins

Harlequin Presents

Her Impossible Baby Bombshell
One Snowbound New Year's Night
Innocent in Her Enemy's Bed

Four Weddings and a Baby

Cinderella's Secret Baby

Jet-Set Billionaires

Cinderella for the Miami Playboy

Signed, Sealed...Seduced

Ways to Ruin a Royal Reputation

The Secret Sisters

Married for One Reason Only
Manhattan's Most Scandalous Reunion

Visit the Author Profile page
at Harlequin.com for more titles.

With deepest gratitude to my editor,
Laurie Johnson, who always seems to know
what questions to ask me when I've literally lost
the plot. Without her savvy navigations, these
characters might have been stuck in the
Bermuda Triangle forever.

PROLOGUE

June, Niagara-on-the-Lake, present day...

IT WAS SUPPOSED to be the happiest day of her life, but Eden Bellamy wasn't happy.

She *should* be. Her groom was a reliable, steady man, exactly like her father. Their marriage would save her father's company. She'd been stressing over how she would do that since Oscar Bellamy's death a year ago. She ought to be thrilled to her pedicured toes that she was finally resolving things.

She pretended she was happy. She plastered a smile on her face as her mother dabbed the corners of her eyes and wished Eden's father was here.

"Me, too, Mama. Go take your seat." *I want this over with.*

Her mother hurried away. Eden's heart seemed to follow, stretching out after her the way a child's might when their mother left them at preschool for the first time. *Wait. Don't leave me. Save me.*

The wedding planner secured the microphone to the sweetheart neckline of her gown and tried to lower Eden's veil. She stopped her.

"I need to see the stairs."

Nerves already had her so unsteady, she feared she would tumble down them. Micah wouldn't let that happen, of course.

Her half brother was standing in as father of the bride. He wore his habitual stoic expression as he stood at the open doors to the terrace watching Quinn, Eden's maid of honor, coax the bridal party into their positions. She urged the flower girl to take the hand of Eden's adolescent cousin as they moved to the top of the stairs for the procession down to the lawn.

"Ready?" The wedding planner finished fussing.

"Is it working?" Eden asked, into the microphone, and heard her own voice come through the speakers outside.

With a pleased smile, the planner melted away. Seconds later, the music paused. The murmuring of the crowd went silent.

Eden's stomach curdled. A dire sense that she was making a colossal mistake condensed around her like a noxious fugue.

He doesn't want you, she silently screamed

at herself, exactly as she had while lying awake last night. As she had every night, in fact, for months. For years.

She tried to recount all the reasons why marrying Hunter Waverly made sense, but her thoughts insistently drifted to that other man, the one who barely acknowledged she existed. The one standing beside Hunter right now.

How could seeing him be the only thing about this day that she looked forward to? She would stand near Remy Sylvain while she spoke her vows to another man and *he wouldn't care*.

Micah held out a crooked arm.

Tears pressed behind her eyes as she came forward to tuck her hand inside his elbow.

Outside, the lyrical notes of the harp invited her to step over the threshold into her new life. Her heart began to pound so forcefully, the microphone might have picked it up. There was a rushing sound in her ears. Her feet tried to glue themselves to the floor.

I can't do this, she thought with abject panic.

"You!" a man's angry voice shouted down below.

It was followed by a plaintive tone from a woman. "Daddy, no! Please!"

"What the hell?" Micah muttered. He strode to the edge of the terrace.

Eden followed and peered down at the hundreds of assembled guests, all facing the pergola where Hunter was standing with his groomsmen and the wedding officiant.

A gray-haired man in rumpled clothes shook his finger at Hunter while his daughter, presumably, tugged his arm, begging him to leave. She held a baby, one new enough that she was protecting its neck as she cuddled it against her shoulder. The senior shook her off and continued berating Hunter.

"Dad!" the woman cried. "He didn't know, okay? I never told him!"

After a stunned pause and a charged exchange between father and daughter, Hunter's voice boomed through the speakers.

"Is it true?"

Eden's brain finally caught up and crashed into what was happening. That old man was claiming the woman's baby was *Hunter's*! Her knees nearly gave out.

Hunter tore off his microphone and handed it to an usher.

That's when she realized Remy was looking up at her.

He was wearing the same morning suit as the rest of the groom's party, but he wore it so much better. His white shirt and burgundy vest with swirls of gold were positively regal on his muscled torso.

If a man was capable of being elegant and beautiful while maintaining every shred of masculinity, that's what Remy managed to do. Always. His hair had been freshly cut into a midfade, his strong jaw shaved clean. His tall, muscled frame was powerful and unmoving, while his demeanor was more remote and contained than ever.

He wasn't shocked by what was going on, though. That's what struck her like a slap. He was watching to see how *she* reacted.

Had he *arranged* this? Had Micah been right? Was Remy willing to ruin her wedding? Her *life*?

Beside her, Micah muttered a string of curses. "I'll kill him. This time, I really will."

Down in the pergola, Remy nudged Hunter. Hunter moved his gaze up to her. So did the woman. Hunter's grim expression hardened with culpability.

The farcical energy crackled for two or three seconds longer, long enough for Eden's heart to twist and wrench inside her chest. Humiliation crept like poison from the pit of her stomach to ache in her cheeks.

The woman with the baby looked equally

mortified. Her expression crumpled and she hurried away.

Eden's numb fingers released her bouquet. It fell off the ledge of the terrace. She dragged her gaze from Remy's unreadable expression and swept herself back into the honeymoon suite of the vineyard's guesthouse.

CHAPTER ONE

Paris, five years ago...

EDEN ALMOST LET Quinn go to the Louvre alone. She had been to the museum before and it was always a crush of people, especially around the most famous painting in the world.

Culture wasn't her priority when she came to Europe. She wanted to visit her brother and enjoy vacation pursuits, like sailing, shopping, swimming and snowboarding.

Quinn liked those things, too, but she hadn't grown up with money. She was building her future on an education obtained through scholarship and maximized every chance to learn.

Eden respected that. In some ways, she envied Quinn her limitless choices. Eden's life path was set in stone. She would finish her business degree, inherit Bellamy Home and Garden and keep it flourishing. She was happy to do so, but she needed a break from the pressure sometimes.

She and Quinn were best friends *because* they were willing to go along with what the other one wanted to do, though. Whether it was homework, browsing boutiques, or craning to catch a glimpse of a painting through a sea of patrons' phone screens, they wanted to hang together and crack dumb jokes for the other's amusement.

"I thought it would be bigger," Quinn said, swaying on her tiptoes.

"Haven't you heard? Size doesn't matter."

It was a lame phrase they threw at each other more often than twelve-year-old boys declared, "That's what she said."

A snort of amusement behind her prompted Eden to glance back.

The breath was stolen clean out of her lungs by a man in distressed denim jeans, suede ankle boots and a mushroom-gray linen jacket over a green shirt with sunflowers on it. His collar was open, revealing a modest gold pendant nestled against the hollow of his brown throat. A protective saint, perhaps.

Confidence radiated off his tall frame. His wide shoulders spoke of physical power. He wore his jacket with the sleeves pushed back, exposing the Montblanc on his wrist. Above his high fade, his black curls were natural and short. His goatee framed his full-lipped mouth. The heavy-lidded gaze that lingered on her sent a gorgeous slithery sensation from her abdomen into places inside her that had never felt alive.

Her cheeks warmed and her breath shortened as she held his rye-whiskey gaze.

"Age matters, though," Quinn mused in her ear.

Eden sent Quinn a side-eye of "shut up" and returned his smile. She was nineteen, definitely old enough to flirt with someone in his midtwenties. This was Paris. It was kind of required by law.

"You speak English?" she asked, which wasn't exactly high-level flirting, but dozens of languages were competing in the din around them. It was a logical opener.

"I do. I'm Canadian. Like you."

"How do you know we're Canadian?" Eden cocked her head with curiosity.

"Halifax is hitting her *r*'s harder than a pirate." He nodded at Quinn. "And you said 'sorry' to the guy who crammed his elbow in your ear."

"Prince Edward Island, thank you," Quinn said, correcting him with mock indignance.

"I'm going to try to get closer." Quinn inserted her shoulder into the crowd.

Eden held out her hand. "Eden. Toronto." She skipped the second *t*, the way most locals did.

"Remy. Montreal." He gave it the Quebecois pronunciation.

They held hands and gazes until Eden was nudged from behind. She took a step into Remy to catch her balance. Her hand pressed one of those sunflowers to his very firm, warm chest. He steadied her with a grip of her elbow.

"Sorry?" she said wryly, trying to cover up how her knees softened at being so close to him. The flutters in her midsection had become waves of heat that pulsed upward into her breasts and throat. Her cheeks were likely turning pink because she was tingling all over with acute warmth.

"No problem." The indent at the corner of his mouth was the most beautiful thing she'd ever seen, but his indulgent gaze was a teensy bit rueful. She heard the reserve in his voice as he released her. "Are you au pairs? Or is this a graduation trip? You don't strike me as backpackers."

He thought she was fresh out of high school? "I come every year to see my brother." She was going for sophistication, but probably came off as boastful. "He keeps an apartment here."

It was more of a penthouse and one of several mansions, villas and top-floor suites that he owned. And, yes, Micah was currently living there. He had arranged their flight and a stupidly generous budget, encouraging her to bring Quinn. Micah was sweet as caramel beneath his titanium crust, but he didn't want to stand around in boutiques debating chartreuse over pistachio-green. "Take both and decide later" had been his impatient contribution to their one and only shopping trip together.

"We're heading back to McGill University in September," Eden clarified.

Remy nodded, his restless gaze scanning her face with a hint of conflict.

Eden could tell he was trying to decide if she was too young for him. She was inexperienced in some ways, but sophisticated in others. She dated regularly, but men her age seemed like juvenile nitwits when compared to her brother, who set a high bar of dynamic intelligence and shouldered far-reaching responsibilities he had inherited too early from his father.

At home, her own father was a big fish in a small pond, but people still acted weird when they found out who he was—sometimes intimidated, other times opportunistic. She sidestepped revealing her male relatives until she got to know strangers better.

"You?" she asked. "Are you on vacation with your wife or…?"

His mouth twitched and his gaze delved more deeply into hers from beneath eyelids that grew heavy with interest.

"I'm single," he assured her. "Here on business, but I have family——" He winced and glanced at his watch. "I'm meeting my cousin, actually. Now I'm late. Are you in Paris long? My friend owns a nightclub. I promised to drop by on Friday. Shall I ask him to put you on the list?" He took out his phone.

"That sounds fun. Eden and Quinn." She didn't give him her last name, not wanting him to look her up. She didn't ask him to include Micah, either. Her brother was already behaving like a Victorian guardian.

"I'll arrive around eleven. Don't let me down. I want to see you again."

His point and wink gave her a sensual kick inside that kept her buzzing for days as she dragged Quinn along the Champs-élysées in search of the perfect dress. She settled on a silver metal-chain dress with a snug halter top and a fringe below the short skirt. Her shoes were four-inch, sequined sandals with straps that spiraled halfway up to her knees.

Quinn picked a strapless green minidress that she chose because it had pockets—big surprise from practical Quinn—but it suited her figure.

When Friday arrived, for once, Quinn wore her gorgeous red hair down, but she was radiating tension on their way to the club.

"Is something wrong?" Eden was so excited she could hardly sit still.

"I'm not sure. I—" She hesitated. Conflict and a desire to evade glinted in her eyes.

Eden prickled with apprehension, but she was distracted by the sign that flashed "Until Dawn" in French.

"That's it. *Jusqu'à l'Aube*," Eden said to Micah's chauffeur and pointed ahead.

"Long line to get in," Quinn noted.

"That means it's popular." Eden had been a tiny bit worried it would be sketchy, but it was in a lively, upscale arrondissement.

The parade of laughing twentysomethings were dressed in chic miniskirts and shiny suits. They sent a mixture of curious and hostile glances when the car stopped at the end of the covered walkway into the nightclub and Eden and Quinn emerged.

"They hate us. Why didn't we get let off at the end?" Quinn asked under her breath.

"We're on The List." At least, they had bet-

ter be. Eden did not want to believe she had
fallen for a scam to boost numbers at a club.
Remy's interest in her had felt as immedi-
ate and strong as hers had been in him. If he
wasn't here, well, she would be more devastated than she was prepared to admit.

She nervously gave their names to the
greeter and they were escorted into the club.
Inside, the crowd bounced to the DJ's pulsing
music beneath flashing colored lights. Their
hostess showed them to the VIP section, where
Remy was holding court on a U-shaped sofa.

He truly was the most gorgeous man. He
rose and flashed a smile, kissing each of her
cheeks as if he was genuinely glad to see her.
As if they were longtime friends. Or something more. He wore black trousers over neon
pink sneakers and a black T-shirt beneath a
blue silk blazer embossed with a pink pais-
ley pattern.

He tried to introduce her and Quinn to his
friends, but all Eden heard was that one was
his cousin from the museum. The woman
wearing long braids and glowing white nail
polish smiled and waved. A couple rose and
motioned that they were headed to the dance
floor. Two men joined them, making room on
the sofa for Eden and Quinn to settle beside
Remy.

"Champagne?" Remy reached for one of the open bottles. "Or rum? Something else?"

They chose champagne and he poured. Eden leaned toward Quinn as she accepted hers. "This must be what it feels like to be rich and famous."

"You are rich and famous," Quinn teased.

"Not like this." This was Micah rich.

Quinn smiled her thanks as she took the glass Remy offered. She waited until Remy had topped up his own and clinked, then sipped.

Eden could hardly keep her glass steady. Her senses were on overload as the crush on the sofa had her pressed tightly against Remy, feeling his every shift and move. As he settled back and set his arm on the back of the sofa, his weight tilted her into him. He smelled as good as he looked, like summer and spice and maybe lust, but that might be her.

Their gazes tangled. She wanted to hear everything he might have to say, but she also wanted to stay exactly like this, simmering in sexual excitement. It was far more intoxicating than any bubbly.

His lips grazed her ear as he dipped his head and asked, "Do you want to dance?"

She nodded and glanced at Quinn. She waved at them to go without her, her mouth pursed in rueful acknowledgment that she was in the way. One of Remy's companions glanced hopefully toward her, but Quinn was already frowning at her phone.

Something *was* bothering her, but Eden's hand was in Remy's and she was too eager to dance. She would question her later.

Remy was so sexy! Being well-dressed, confident and wealthy wasn't enough for him. He danced well, too, sinking into the groove while his hands shaped the air around her. He rolled his body and kept his gaze fixed on her, making her feel like the most desirable woman alive.

She loved dancing. Nothing made her feel more beautiful than becoming one with the music—except possibly brushing up against Remy's chest and thigh, feeling his hand graze her arm and lower back and hip. He brought her hand up over her head and twirled her, then she backed into him, thrilling when he slid his hands down her sides.

This wasn't dancing. It was foreplay. She had kissed and messed around a little, but always in an experimental way, never feeling this level of potent attraction. Her desire to be closer and touch more of him, to press herself into him, was such a force, she thought she would burst from it.

When someone stumbled into her, the spell was nearly broken. Remy quickly drew her off the dance floor into a shadowed corner at the end of the bar, brow furrowed in concern. His touch skimmed down her arm as he leaned close.

"Are you okay?"

"Fine."

Now she was entranced by how their heads were tilted close, their lips *so* close.

Acting purely on instinct, she slid her hand up his shoulder and pressed lightly in invitation. His hand splayed on her waist, drawing her in.

She held her breath as the press of their bodies clicked like magnets connecting. A sensation of rightness, of completion, encompassed her as their lips met and slid, parted and sealed.

Joy blossomed within her. He was The One. She knew it from the way his arms closed around her in a way that was both gentle and powerful, crushing her into him in the most tender way. Claiming, but telling her she was precious and important.

With the colored lights glinting behind her closed eyelids and the thumping music amplifying her heartbeat, she transcended her human self. For a few seconds, they occupied one common dimension of time and space.

There was nothing between them but sparking electricity and acute pleasure. It was perfect. Utterly perfect.

And so hot. She leaned into him a little more. His hand splayed over her bottom and his tongue tagged hers. She twined her arms around his neck and—

He jerked back a step, releasing her so abruptly she staggered to regain her balance. In the same second, he swung around to confront someone.

No. He'd been pulled, she realized. Dragged into a confrontation that quickly turned into a shoving match, one that might have turned to blows, but she suddenly recognized who had attacked him.

"Micah!" she cried in horror. "Stop!"

CHAPTER TWO

Last October...

TONIGHT WAS THEIR coming-out as a couple.

Hunter's sister, Vienna, had introduced Eden to Hunter Waverly last month. They'd begun dating very casually. He was preoccupied by a court case that had threatened his national telecom business, Wave-Com, but the final judgment had come down a few days ago. Hunter was throwing a splashy soiree to celebrate his win and he wanted Eden by his side.

"I want people to know we're serious. You've stuck beside me through a rough time. That bodes well for our future."

Did he think she had so many prospects that dating him had been an act of loyalty? Given the jeopardy at her own family company, she was actually a liability. She had to come clean before things went any further.

"I don't want to misrepresent myself," she

told him haltingly. "I need you to understand what you're getting into before you we talk about whether we have a future."

Eden had studied hard to prepare herself to take the reins at Bellamy Home and Garden. She had worked in the storefront at fourteen and moved to an entry-level position at head office when she turned sixteen. Through university, she had taken on greater responsibilities, running marketing campaigns and negotiating buyer agreements and working on inclusion policies with HR.

She had believed she had earned the respect of the board along the way. When her father had passed, she had thought she had everyone's support as the next president of BH&G.

Knives had promptly come out, however. She discovered that movements toward a coup had begun when her father's health had declined. As economic storms had battered the company, a handful of acquisitive shareholders had injected capital with a ticking-time-bomb sort of clause. If they didn't earn a guaranteed return by the end of next year, they would assume controlling interest.

They were already trying to oust Eden. If she didn't fight with every cell of her being, her family's legacy would be a pitiful headline bemoaning the demise of "another" Canadian institution. All options were on the table, including an arranged marriage.

"That's why I let Vienna introduce us. I didn't want to bring it up when you were battling your own dragons, but I can't keep quiet about it any longer."

Hunter listened with equanimity. "I do have experience with dragons," he said dryly, having just triumphed over one. "I'm sure we can work out a win-win."

For the first time in a long time, Eden allowed herself a shred of optimism. Her smile was natural as she stood next to Hunter, greeting his guests. Maybe she wasn't in love with him, but she had every reason to believe she *could* love him. Eventually.

Not a frothy, heart-twisting infatuation, either. She didn't want that awful thing that continued to strike a pang of yearning through her soul. Whatever she had *thought* she had felt that long-ago night in Paris had been a deliberate play by a scoundrel on her youthful pheromones. It hadn't been real so it shouldn't haunt her.

It did, though. *He* did. Every man was measured against that illusion, even Hunter. He was the first to come close, but even he was found wanting for the crime of not being *him*. Worse, even the times she did feel a smidge

of curiosity about a man, she felt so humiliated by her gullibility, she didn't trust her own
judgment.

If Vienna hadn't set them up, she wouldn't
have trusted Hunter. Even then, she had made
it clear she wanted to take things slow. They
hadn't had sex and probably wouldn't until
they were married. Hunter said he was fine
with that.

Maybe if he had lit her fire the way Remy
had, she might have lost her virginity by now,
but the only man who had ever made her crave
sex was her brother's mortal enemy.

It was confusing and made her wonder if
she possessed some hidden kink that yearned
for the forbidden.

"There he is," Hunter said with warm affection, excusing them from their conversation
with a couple from New York and drawing
her toward a man that made her entire body
feel as though it iced over, became heavy and
unwieldy.

"Eden, this is Remy Sylvain. Eden Bel-
lamy," Hunter introduced, then added to Remy,
"You'll remember I said Vi was setting me up?
Turns out she has a talent for matchmaking."

Somehow, Remy had become even more
freaking handsome. More mesmerizing. His
beard was a narrow strip on his chin, his hair

shorter, his face now more mature in the nearly five years since she'd met him so briefly in Paris. He still had obscenely great fashion sense, wearing a closely tailored suit in dark merlot over a black shirt and tie.

The flash of his dark gold gaze cut across her like a scythe, practically taking her knees out from beneath her. "It's nice to meet you." His voice was cool. He offered his hand.

As it penetrated that he was pretending they had never met, she placed her limp hand in his, clammy skin burning on contact with his hot palm.

A lifetime of cultivated manners had the words "It's nice to meet you, too" slipping from her lips. It wasn't nice. It was a deadly shock. How was no one noticing that her jaw had fallen onto the floor?

He shook her hand in a perfunctory way. Not hurtful, but she felt his hardness toward her before he released her, as though *she* had burned *him*.

She *felt* hurt, which was so stupid! She didn't want to feel anything for him or about him, least of all rejected. He hadn't truly wanted her in the first place.

Her mind raced, trying to work out whether he would blurt something out in front of

Hunter. Should she say something? She had only just gotten her life back on track!

She couldn't speak, anyway. Her heart was in her throat, cutting off her voice. Her breasts tightened and her cheeks were on fire.

The memory of Paris was detonating in her mind, but so was Micah's insistence afterward that she should *forget it happened.*

Also, Hunter hated scenes. His stepmother was notorious for them. He would dump her if he knew what a drama had unfolded back then. Eden would be back to square one, looking for a husband who possessed enough scratch— and enough courage—to save her company.

Her stomach knotted in anticipation of Remy saying something, but he kept his expression neutral and polite.

"Congratulations on the win," he said to Hunter, exchanging a more heartfelt handshake and shoulder squeeze with him. "You deserve it."

"Thanks. How's your family? Is Yasmine still in New York?"

Eden stood there in a fog, waiting for Remy to look her in the eye again while he and Hunter briefly caught up. Remy turned his head her way a couple of times, appearing to include her in the conversation, but he looked through her every time.

He was really pretending they were strangers! Even though his lips had been on hers. His hands had fondled her backside. She had felt his erection against her stomach.

The backs of her eyes stung and her heart pounded so hard she nearly swayed under the impact. It was Hunter's night, though. This wasn't the time or place to confront Remy about old wounds.

Why did those wounds feel so *fresh*?

"I hate to be the guy who fails to stick around for the toasts, but I have commitments elsewhere. I'll say hello to Vienna before I go, though." Remy scanned the room. "I'm happy you're finally able to put this behind you."

"Thank you. Us, too. Let's get a beer soon. I'll put Vienna on the hunt. We can double-date." It was pure facetiousness on Hunter's part and spoke to how close the men were that he would make a joke like that.

"Sure." Remy made a tight noise that held no actual humor.

Was she the only one who'd noticed? That cynical scrape of sound made her heart shrink in her chest.

"I'll text you," Remy said to Hunter, sending another streak of apprehension through Eden. He added an absent nod in Eden's direction before he slipped through the crowd to the other side of the room.

They were quickly approached by someone else, but Eden was distracted. She couldn't imagine a more hurtful way for Remy to behave toward her. At least if he'd been angry or hurled accusations, she would have known he felt something toward her, even if it was hatred. His cool disinterest only confirmed what Micah had told her—that Remy had been using her as a tool of spite.

"Okay?" Hunter asked, perhaps noticing her silence.

"Tiny headache. I'll be fine," she assured him with a wan smile.

She felt sick, though. Her inner radar tracked Remy for the next half hour before he waved at Hunter on his way to the exit.

Hunter nodded and Remy melted away.

As much as his presence here had turned this party into a pressure cooker of anticipating disaster, now she felt bereft. Why? Why did she have to feel this way about someone she had only met three times? Someone who had cared absolutely nothing about her?

She lurched her way through the rest of the evening, mind churning with trying to work out whether she should tell Hunter that she had once kissed Remy in Paris.

At face value, it sounded laughably innocent. A kiss stopped by a protective older brother. The night had been more embarrassing than anything. It wasn't as if she'd given him her virginity or shared her deepest held secrets.

Micah had acted as though Remy had attacked her, though. He had shoved him and Remy had shoved back. Micah had made threats. Not the kind that communicated, "Ha-ha, I'll kill you if you touch my sister." No. Micah had been dead serious and things might have become truly violent if Eden hadn't thrown herself between them. Quinn had rushed up to grab Micah's arm. It had been *awful*.

Micah had never fully explained what had happened, only insisting that Remy had targeted her to strike at him. *We have history. It's not your fault. Forget this ever happened.* When Eden got home to Toronto and brought it up with her mother, Lucille had been distraught, but also very cryptic. *Just leave it, pet.*

Eden had spent years trying to forget. She had concentrated on finishing school, worked alongside her father, cared for him and buried him, taking over at Bellamy Home and Garden after he was gone.

Now BH&G was hanging by a thread. As

Hunter drove her home after the party, she tentatively asked, "How do you know Remy?"

"University. We shared some classes and a similar life experience, I guess. We were both taking over our respective empires. We don't have time to see much of each other these days, but it's one of those friendships where we pick up where we left off. I expect he'll be the best man at our wedding."

Her stomach tensed as if receiving a blow. His words sent her mind tilting off-kilter while the streetlamps flickered in her eyes.

Say something, she urged herself. *Say something now.* But she didn't want to malign his best friend. Was that why Remy had pretended he didn't know her? To protect Hunter finding out how low he could sink?

What if Remy turned it around and made it about her and Micah? Would he see this relationship as another chance to take a swipe at her brother?

"Am I rushing you?" Hunter asked with quiet caution. "I thought that's what we meant when we said we were serious."

"No. Um, I mean, a little. You caught me by surprise." She tried to brush away her misgivings and not ruin the opportunity before her. With a tremulous smile that was equal parts hope and trepidation, she said, "I would love to hear what you're proposing."

His mouth quirked at her pun. A few days later, he presented a detailed business proposal that included a prenuptial agreement.

That brought Micah flying into town, which worked for Eden. She cornered him before they left to meet Hunter for dinner.

"I should tell you something before we go. Hunter knows Remy Sylvain."

"I know." Micah slipped his phone into his pocket, giving her his full attention. His expression had hardened to granite.

"Did you have Hunter investigated?" she hissed with outrage.

"The Waverlys have skeletons falling out of every second closet. Of course, I peeked in the open ones." He shrugged, not the least bit remorseful. "Waverly and Sylvain are school friends. Aside from a weekend golfing last summer, they rarely see one another. They don't have financial ties. I don't think Sylvain is conspiring with Waverly to use you to get at me, if that's what you're worried about."

It had crossed her mind and she hated that she had become so mistrustful.

"There's nothing for Waverly to gain by that," Micah continued in his detached tone. "He needs the appearance of stability and wholesomeness that you bring to this union as much as you need his cash. A fresh scandal is the very last thing he wants. I'm confident he's acting in good faith, but I'll say again, you don't *have* to marry him."

She held up her hand, forestalling that heavily belabored argument.

"Just tell me one thing. Does Mama's refusal to let me accept *your* money have anything to do with the feud between you and Remy?"

"Not really."

"A little?"

"Look." His eyebrows settled into a line of frustrated concern. "I knew your father was having money troubles a few years ago. I offered to help. Mama asked me to stay out of it. I understand her aversion to taking my father's money. His parents always believed she got pregnant on purpose and married him for his wealth. She refuses to fuel that misconception. I respect that, but you're in charge of BH and G now. You can make a different decision."

She sighed, wishing she could, but their mother had already told her she would rather lose the company than save it with Micah's father's money. Eden thought Lucille was taking pride a little too far, but she also wanted to respect their mother's wishes.

"And Remy? Why does he hate you?"

Micah hissed out a sigh. "Remy's father worked for mine. He stole proprietary information for our competitor."

"Industrial espionage?" Eden thought that was something that only happened in films.

"There was gossip that he was retaliating for an affair between my father and Remy's mother. All sides denied that and Remy's father has always claimed he was robbed. My father was never able to prove that he was paid to steal the schematics, but he moved his family to Canada and started an airline. You do the math."

"Okay." She took in that information and saw the bad blood it would create. "But that's history between your father and his. Why do *you* hate *him*?"

"He went after *you*."

Her heart lurched in remembered anguish.

"Don't you think…?" She felt self-conscious even saying it. "Isn't it possible we met by accident and he actually liked me?"

"No, Eden, I don't." Micah's voice was gentle, but heavy with reluctant truth, which made it all the more awful to hear. With another sigh, he hung his hands on his hips. "You remember when I was supposed to come live here? I started school and all the rest?"

"Yes."

"There was an incident with Remy back then. I don't want to get into it. It was kid stuff, but my father overreacted. As he was wont to do." His expression darkened. "The bottom line is, I knew it was between the two of them and let it go. Remy hasn't. Years have gone by and we have both taken over our respective companies, but do you think his will entertain a bid from us for any of their projects? Never." He sliced his hand through the air. "And that's fine. I don't care if he wants to be petty. I don't need work that badly, but a few weeks before that night in Paris, I bought a vineyard his family had been trying to purchase. I didn't know that. I was in the right place at the right time with the right price. He was obviously annoyed and *that's* why he went after you."

She hugged herself, stung afresh by the thought of being used.

"Should I tell Hunter all of that?"

"*I'll* tell him what he needs to know, which is that if he wants to marry you, he needs to find a different best man."

"Oh, *don't*." Panic stung her veins. She wasn't sure why. She told herself it was anxiety that the feud would only escalate, but it was more insidious than that. She didn't want to push Remy away. Deep down where she barely wanted to acknowledge her desires, she wanted to see him again.

"Let's be adults," she urged. "If Remy is prepared to act as if he doesn't know me—"

"You've seen him?"

"Briefly. And I don't want to sabotage what I have with Hunter by making him choose between me and his friend."

"You're determined to marry him, then?"

"Hunter?" *Of course, Hunter.* "Yes." She lifted her chin, trying to sound confident when she was still a scattered mess. "If he'll have me."

"Do you love him?"

"Not yet." She bit her lip. "Do you think that's bad?"

Micah snorted. "Romantic love is a pretty bow people put on things like desire for sex and fear of death. This kind of caring is what matters." He pointed between them and tucked his chin to send her a look of exasperated affection. "I will always look out for your best interests. I want you to be comfortable and content. I believe this marriage—not Hunter, per se, but the marriage he's proposing—will meet your needs. I'm glad you're going into it with a practical mindset rather than telling me you can't live without him. In that respect, it's good that you're not in love with him."

"Thanks, I guess," she said dryly.

"His poor taste in friends concerns me, though. I'll keep a close eye on Sylvain. If he steps one millimeter out of line..." He left the threat hanging.

In the end, she told Hunter a pale version of the truth.

"I met Remy years ago at a nightclub. It was one dance so I'm not surprised he didn't recognize me. He and Micah aren't on the friendliest of terms, though. I didn't want to make anything of it, especially at your party."

"I appreciate that," Hunter said solemnly. "I've had enough scenes in my life."

He seemed to let it go, but a few days later, Hunter said, "I spoke with Remy. He said his beef with Micah is firmly in the past. He doesn't want to revisit it, which is why he acted as though he didn't know you. He offered to drop out of the wedding if there's a conflict."

"Don't be silly. It's your wedding, too! You should have the best man you want." What was *wrong* with her? She didn't want to see Remy again. Did she?

If that was her motive, she was disappointed. He only appeared once before the wedding, at the engagement party.

Eden thought she had adequately braced

herself to see him again, but the second he came into the room—before she even saw him with her eyes—a tingling sensation prickled across her skin.

She looked up and he was looking right at her.

The ground fell away. She was both soaring and plummeting, hot and cold, happy and aching with loss.

Once again, he was devilishly handsome and painfully indifferent. Once again, he made his excuses as he arrived.

"I'm flying to Martinique tonight, but I wanted to extend my well-wishes." He didn't kiss her cheek the way everyone else had, only shook her hand very briefly.

She closed her fist around the sensation to keep it lingering on her palm.

"We should honeymoon in Martinique," Hunter said, glancing at her.

Did Remy flinch? "Rainy season starts in June."

"Right. Forgot about that. Niagara Falls, then, since we'll be in the neighborhood." Hunter winked. It was a joke. Micah had already offered his island villa in Greece. "We're marrying at Niagara-on-the-Lake," Hunter explained to Remy.

"Oh?" Remy's tone was impossible to decipher, but it was weighted with…something. Remy held Hunter's gaze and Remy's eyes narrowed with— Eden couldn't tell what that was. Significance. A question?

Hunter's face went oddly blank. Something in the exchange made the back of Eden's neck prickle, but Hunter glanced at her.

"It was Eden's decision." Hunter was inviting her to fill in the blanks.

"Oh. Um, my aunt has a vineyard there." Eden's voice was thin and unsteady. Hopefully, the men attributed it to bridal nerves. "Weddings are her specialty." And it was the Bellamy family brand that they support Canadian merchants whenever possible.

"Do you have a lot of family attending?" Remy's hammered-gold irises flashed a spark into her eyes that left them stinging. A hot sensation filled her chest and swam up to her throat, suffocating her words.

"Most of my relations live in the Greater Toronto Area. My brother bases himself in Berlin these days." She fought to steady her tone. "He'll step in as father of the bride."

She waited, ears straining for Remy's reaction.

The silence went on a beat too long.

Hunter must have misread the thinness in her tone. His warm hand squeezed her shoulder. "I'm still kicking myself that I didn't call you right after Vienna suggested setting us up. Maybe I could have met him. Oscar Bellamy sounds like he was a good man."

It was her cue to say her father would have liked him, but she could only manage a weak smile. Her father never would have asked her to marry to save the company. He had fallen for her mother the minute he met her and waited as long as he had to.

"I'm sorry for your loss," Remy said distantly. His gaze flicked to Hunter's hand on her shoulder, then slipped past her. His cheek ticked. "I should say hello to Vienna."

Vienna is married, Eden wanted to scream for no particular reason at all.

"I'm arranging my own bachelor party. My PA is," Hunter said, correcting himself with a wry cant of his head. "Golf in the Okanagan. I'll have her send you the dates."

"Wouldn't miss it," Remy said with a tight smile. One final, flashing glance landed on her before he nodded and walked away.

Her brother had already said he wouldn't be back until the wedding, but Eden could have wept at the strain that continued to hold her taut. This felt like a twisted game of chicken, where Remy was calling her bluff, waiting to see if she would go through with marrying

Hunter while she waited to see if he would interfere and disrupt it.

As the weeks toward the wedding counted down, she began to believe that Remy would let the wedding happen. She needed this marriage so she ought to have been relieved. She only grew more anxious.

When Remy missed the wedding rehearsal at the vineyard, the night before the wedding, she asked Hunter with as much levity as she could muster, "Are you sure the rings will arrive on time?"

"I have them. Remy texted. He's running late, but he's on the road. He'll arrive tonight. Everything will go smoothly tomorrow. I promise."

She smiled as if she believed him, but a jagged lump sat in her chest.

The lump stayed there, behind her breastbone, right up until the wedding planner said, "Ready?"

CHAPTER THREE

Present day

"EDEN—" VIENNA CAME into the suite behind her.

Eden whirled on her. "Is it *true*?"

Her voice reverberated through the speakers outside.

Quinn, ever the protective friend and efficient maid of honor, made a cutting gesture across her own throat. She unclipped the microphone the wedding planner had attached to Eden's neckline and turned it off, setting it amid the clutter that had collected on the bar.

"I don't know." Vienna's expression was a study in apology and distress. "I honestly wouldn't be surprised if our stepmother staged this. She's that spiteful."

As Eden's heart took a swoop between anguish and hope, she looked to Quinn. Quinn was as supportive as ever, but even though her expression brimmed with empathy, she shook her head, indicating this development was a death knell as far as she was concerned.

Micah finished shuffling the bridesmaids off the terrace and through the suite, instructing the teenager to deliver the flower girl to her parents before he closed the doors.

He folded his arms and cocked one dark eyebrow in a silent "I can still help you."

Any second, Lucille would burst in to keep Eden from agreeing to exactly that. If she had allowed Eden to accept Micah's help in the first place, she wouldn't be in this situation!

I need this marriage. It was the mantra Eden had used to muffle all the misgivings she'd had from the time Hunter had proposed to this morning, when she'd struggled to keep her breakfast down.

Why? Evil stepmother notwithstanding, Hunter was perfect. He was even-tempered and smart, wealthy and good-looking. He understood she had responsibilities and aspirations and was ready to support her in achieving them without trying to tell her how to do it. He wanted a family.

She clenched her eyes over a hot sting.

Judging by five seconds ago, he *had* a family. A baby he had abandoned, if the accusations by the baby's grandfather were to be believed.

The young mother had said something about not telling him. Hunter wasn't one to wear his emotions on his sleeve, but his astonishment had been apparent, as had the fact he recognized the woman.

Has he been having an affair all this time? Am I still that blind and stupid?

Eden started to rub her eye before she remembered the makeup that had taken an hour for a professional artist to apply.

Was this even happening? Or was she in one of those too-real dreams brought on by anticipation of a big day? No matter where she was traveling, she always had a missed-my-flight nightmare right before her alarm went off. Maybe that's all this was.

She pinched her arm with her manicured nails, trying to awaken. Trying to convince herself she was sleeping late because she had tossed and turned past midnight, consumed with thoughts of *him*.

Curse Remy Sylvain! He hadn't been surprised by any of this. As she'd stood out there, aghast at the scene unfolding below her, the groom's *best man* had only lifted an inscrutable look to *her*.

"Let me help you out of this," Quinn said

gently as she brushed aside the train on the layers of satin and tulle skirts that Eden wore.

Eden stiffened. "I can't change until I know whether it's true."

"You still want to marry him?" Micah's voice thundered with astonishment. *"Let me help you."*

"No." Eden thrust out her palm in a halt against the suggestion. "If you want to argue about that, go do it with Mama. In fact, go head her off. I don't want her in here." Was she blaming Lucille for this fiasco? Perhaps a little. She would also start to cry if her mother came in and wrapped her arms around her. She would ruin makeup, dress and day all in one go. "Tell everyone to stay calm. This is just a delay." *Please, God.*

Micah's eyebrows went up. He was not used to being ordered around, but Eden would play the bridezilla card as long as she could cling to it.

I need this marriage.

As the door closed behind him, Eden looked to Vienna. "Has he been seeing her all this time?"

Vienna's head went back with indignation on her brother's behalf.

"If he has, it's news to me. *When?* He was wrapped up in the court case, then you two started dating..." Vienna's defensiveness trailed off as she squinted into the middle distance. "He was here with Remy last summer, though, for a weekend of golf. That was before I introduced you two. Maybe he met her then?"

To Eden's eternal damnation, the lurch in her stomach had nothing to do with her groom picking up women on a bro weekend. It twisted and shrank because Remy probably had as well.

Why? She was nearly twenty-five, but she was more obsessed with that vexing man than a preteen with a celebrity crush.

"The baby looked pretty young," Vienna said hesitantly. "Maybe six or eight weeks?"

"That math checks out," Quinn said with a pained nod, equally reluctant to crush Eden's hopes and dreams.

"I'll find out what I can. You can't stand here wondering." Vienna slipped away.

"And then there were two," Quinn murmured as she brought across one of the mimosas that had been delivered a few hours ago. "I'm sorry this is happening, Eden. Really sorry. But you wouldn't marry him if he has a baby with someone else, would you?"

"Maybe?" Eden sipped. The tepid liquid dripped like battery acid down the back of her throat. "Not if he's been with her all this time, but he looked pretty shocked. If it was just a—a fling and he only found out today…" She could hear herself reaching for justifications that would allow her to forgive him.

I need this marriage.

"It's not the way I planned to start our family, but we both want one." Her voice was strained by the growing tightness in her throat.

Had they wanted a family with each other, though? It struck her that Hunter had been as content as she was to put off sex, despite the ten months that had passed while they dated and became engaged. They had shared a few long kisses, which had been pleasant enough. Not earth-shattering, but warm enough she had thought sleeping with him wouldn't be a chore.

She hadn't really *wanted* to sleep with him, though. Not the way she *really* wanted—

"That's bargaining," Quinn noted quietly.

"Pardon?"

"The stages of grief aren't just for grief. A stalled car can trigger them and you're going through them now. You don't want to believe the baby is his because that means the wedding has to be called off. That's disbelief and denial. Now you're trying to tell yourself there's a way to make his baby fit into your life so the marriage can go ahead. It can't, Eden. I'm sorry, but it can't."

Eden clenched her eyes shut against her friend's kind but firm truth-telling.

"It's not like he's had a baby all along and you knew what you were getting," Quinn continued, saying what Eden knew, but didn't really want to hear. "The conditions have changed. At the very least, you need time to revisit the terms of your marriage before you go ahead with it. This wedding can't happen today."

"I don't *have* time," Eden cried.

"I know," Quinn noted with a frustrating level of patience and understanding.

"You have never supported this marriage," she accused Quinn, hearing herself resorting to anger, but Quinn didn't take it personally and maintained her calm tone.

"I don't support marriage as a concept. It's not personal to you and Hunter. I want you to have what you want, Eden—I do. But this isn't it. Not anymore."

"I need this marriage," Eden sobbed and swirled away in a rustle of tulle. The first few times she had picked up all these skirts, it had been like gathering clouds and dreams. Now they felt like heavy armloads of soiled laundry.

"Would your mother support you going to these lengths?" Quinn prodded gently. "Now? After this?"

"Go ask her!" Eden waved her hand in vexation. "I think there's more to her stubbornness than pride, but the fact she won't talk about Micah's father tells me more than if she did."

"What do you mean?" Quinn frowned.

"I've always suspected…" Eden hesitated to voice her ugly suspicion, hating to think of it. "I think Micah's father was abusive, but I can't ask her that. I can't ask Micah."

Quinn recoiled slightly and hugged herself, mouth somber and gaze dropping to the floor. "No," she replied. "I can see why you don't want to push her to speak about that."

Maybe her reasoning was more emotionally driven than logical, but Eden was grateful Quinn understood and supported her refusal to press her mother to talk of something so potentially painful.

There was a knock on the door that turned both of their heads.

"Eden, it's me," Hunter said.

Quinn's cheeks went hollow. She moved to let him in, stepping out to give them privacy.

"It's bad luck to see the bride before the wedding," Eden said, hearing the hysteria creeping into her tone. It was moving like poison through her arteries and nerve branches and lung tissue because one look at his grim expression and she knew. She knew it was true. She knew she wasn't getting married today.

In reaction, promises and assurances and angry retaliations burbled out of her. Very little of what she said was the result of having a spurned heart. She was humiliated, yes, but the acrid taste in her mouth was failure. She was not going to save her father's company today.

The iconic chain that her great-grandfather had started as a mail-order catalog of bulbs and seeds, the one that supplied middle-class families across the country with their home-and-garden needs, would gasp its last breath on her watch.

That was more shame than she was prepared to accept.

Hunter didn't stand there and let her berate him. He cut into her litany with a firm "I'm sorry," and walked out.

Quinn came back in as Eden was still swaying in shock, too devastated to even cry.

"Let me help you—" Quinn began.

"Go tell Micah to send everyone home. Or— They should eat the food, right?" She was now in the stage of trying to keep everything normal despite the fact a nuclear-size catastrophe had landed in her lap. "They've come all this way."

"I'm sure the wedding planner has dealt with

things like this before," Quinn said soothingly. "I'll have an announcement made, then I'll come back to help you change."

Eden nodded and knocked back the last of her mimosa, brain firing with fight-or-flight chemicals. Mostly flight. She hated herself so much in this moment, she wanted to crawl out of her own skin. There was no way she could face all those guests, who would cast pitying looks at her.

She set down the champagne glass and reached for another, but noticed the fob on the bar with its I-heart-PEI key chain.

She didn't overthink it. Her purse was right there, her phone on the charger beside it. She scrambled everything into her bag and opened the door to the hall.

"Eden," her mother called. Lucille was coming into the suite from the terrace.

Eden ignored her and rushed out, sweeping down the inside stairs.

The voices in the breakfast room silenced as she appeared, but she didn't so much as glance to see who was gathered there. She shot out the main doors to the path lined with tall hedges that led to the guesthouse parking lot.

It was a dirty trick to steal her friend's car and not even wait for Quinn to catch up and

come with her, but her friend would understand.

Eden burst from the path, already scanning
for Quinn's blue hatchback—

Tires screeched and the nose of a black
sports car huffed a breath against her volumi-
nous skirts. The engine growled dangerously.

Eden hadn't even looked for cars before running straight out in front of this one. She was
the proverbial deer in the headlights—para-
lyzed, unable to make sense of her own dis-
torted reflection in the windshield.

The tinted window lowered on the driv-
er's side. Remy's carved mahogany expression glared at her. Her heart was pounding so
loudly, she barely heard his growled command.

"Get in."

CHAPTER FOUR

THROUGH THE OPEN window of his car, Remy heard voices in the distance, near the entrance to the tasting room. They grew more animated the longer Eden stood before him.

Eden glanced in that direction and horror solidified on her expression as she realized she was about to be spotted and photographed. She scrambled to open his passenger door and dropped into the low seat with an "Oof."

Then she gathered—and gathered—her billowing skirts into her lap, like piling snow for a snow fort.

"Is that it?" he asked testily when she finally dragged the door shut. His veins were still on fire at nearly striking her with his car.

"Would you get me out of here?" She reached for her seat belt.

No. That's what he ought to be saying. How the words *get in* had passed his lips was a mystery he wasn't ready to unravel. Fate and karma were not concepts he subscribed to, but his mother had always been very philosophical about life unfolding the way it was meant to. Given the way Eden kept landing in front of him, he was beginning to understand his own helplessness against such greater forces.

He finished making his way out of the smaller parking lot to the main one, crawling now instead of lighting up his tires because mad women were darting out of hedges.

At the exit to the main road, a Mercedes-Benz SUV turned out ahead of a handful of midsize vehicles. Remy assumed that was Hunter, leaving with Amelia, chased by paparazzi.

Remy had made a handful of executive decisions in the moments following Amelia's appearance. While the guests had been gasping at the accusations leveled by Amelia's father, Remy had been calculating the age of the infant she held. Hunter didn't kiss and tell—or make a habit of one-night stands—but Remy distinctly remembered the smoldering heat coming off the pair as he and Hunter had shared drinks with Amelia and her friend last summer. Remy had taken Amelia's friend home, allowing nature to take its course between the other two.

Apparently, nature had gone all the way. Amelia's baby was almost certainly Hunter's.

And, because Remy knew Hunter would never abandon his child, Remy had instantly known the wedding was off.

Firmly ignoring any personal feelings on the matter, Remy had done his duty as Hunter's best man. He had instructed the wedding planner to open the bar while they waited for the official announcement. He had ensured that the food would be served on time and the band would play their sets as scheduled. He quietly suggested to Hunter's grandfather that he take Amelia's father for a drink, since they were likely to be in-laws very soon.

Then, when he glimpsed Hunter wearing a grim expression as he headed purposefully toward the guesthouse, Remy had searched out Vienna, who gave him a grave little nod of confirmation. *She looks just like him.*

Remy informed Vi that everything was under control and urged her to call him if he could help in any way, but explained he had commitments elsewhere.

He didn't. Only the ones he had fabricated so he could leave the wedding as soon as politely possible, but he sensed Micah Gould wanted to pin blame for today's farce on him.

Remy had some hard truths he would love

to hurl at Micah, but Remy had promised his father he would keep his lips sealed on all of it. He decided to get the hell out of Dodge before he had a run-in with Micah, or did something equally stupid and spoke to Eden.

Even though he had a thousand questions for her. He had bones to pick, and accusations and defensive explanations he shouldn't feel an urge to make because his family was the one that had been wronged.

Or so he had told himself many times, especially in the last few months.

He turned in the opposite direction from the SUV and glanced at her, biting back a compulsion to ask if she was okay. She absolutely was not. She was pallid beneath her golden-brown complexion, eyes wide with shock.

But she was still so beautiful, she punched the breath out of him.

Eden Bellamy had entranced him from the first time he'd glimpsed her, flashing a dimple as she made a cheeky remark to her friend.

Remy had been killing a few minutes until meeting his cousin, who worked in one of the other departments of the Louvre. It had always been his game with himself to see how close he could get to the *Mona Lisa* without having to jostle through the crowd. He had never once arrived at the rope, but on that day, five years ago, he hadn't even glanced toward the painting. He'd been too enamored with the mysterious smile on the face that turned to regard him.

Eden was classically beautiful—he couldn't overlook that—but a gentle warmth radiated from her that he found even more compelling. On that day, she had worn a filmy summer dress that gave her figure the grace of a goddess in a glen.

Two nights later, she had delivered a heart punch when she turned up at a nightclub in a sparkling silver dress. Her hair had been a wild mass of glossy black ringlets falling around her elegant cheekbones. She'd been all legs and sensuous movements, eyes smoky and her entire being held together with an air of self-possession.

As fantasy-provoking as she'd been, Remy was very careful in how he treated women. They were not objects. He didn't make assumptions about their interest beyond a dance and a laugh. When she had leaned into him in a shadowed corner, however, and offered her mouth, he had greedily devoured her lips.

He'd been lost in a way he had never experienced, not before or since. He still avoided reliving that memory, however. It was too raw, switching so abruptly from all-encompassing passion to near violence. From acute pleasure to toxic aggression.

Things had come so close to violence, the music had been stopped. Bouncers had immobilized him and Micah. The fact that Remy's friend owned the nightclub was the only reason the police hadn't been called. They had both been asked to leave.

Remy was still stinging with affront and injustice at the way Micah's lip had curled in derision as he'd told Eden, "He's using you to get at me."

"How?" The accusation hadn't made sense. "Are you *with* him?" Remy was immediately appalled that they had locked lips. In those confused seconds, he felt he'd been set up and betrayed. Self-loathing had had him spitting out the taste of her lingering on his tongue.

"He's my *brother*." Eden recoiled from the suggestion that she and Micah were romantically involved.

Micah's sister? Even worse. Remy's heart lurched with agonized disappointment, a reaction that made even less sense. He searched Eden's features, not seeing much resemblance. Micah was distinctly white European, while Eden looked mixed-race.

In looking for the resemblance between them, Remy had become morbidly fascinated by the shape of Micah's nose and mouth and jawline. It churned up a different recognition, one that was knotted up with helpless anger and defensiveness. Apprehension that the secret he kept so diligently could be discovered if he spent any time with them.

"Don't pretend you didn't know she's my sister," Micah accused contemptuously.

Culpability at what he *did* know must have flashed onto Remy's face.

Micah misinterpreted it, and warned viciously, "Stay away from her."

He collected Eden and her wide-eyed friend. They disappeared from the club and his life.

Remy had breathed a sigh of relief on one score, but he had never fully shaken his memory of Eden. His desire for her. He'd been compelled to look her up and learned that she was a Bellamy, only related to Micah because her mother had briefly been married to Micah's father, Kelvin Gould. Lucille had remarried when she moved back to Canada.

If Remy had known Eden was associated with the Gould family, he never would have spoken to her. He had sworn to himself he never would again.

At least, that's what he'd told himself. Yet here he was, inviting her into his car today.

A muted buzzing sounded within the folds

of her skirt. She fished through yards of netting and silk to reveal her purse, and opened it. As she glanced at the screen on her phone, she made a helpless noise then swiped to accept a video call.

"Where *are* you?" It sounded like her friend Quinn. Her voice was high and anxious.

"I had to get out of there. Tell everyone I'm okay—" She shot Remy a look as though it had just occurred to her that she might not be able to trust him.

As if *his* family was the dangerous one.

"Whose car is that?" Quinn asked with surprise.

"Um." Eden swallowed, then asked tentatively, "Is anyone else there with you?"

"Do not tell me she's with him." Micah's outrage was tangible enough to reach through the phone and ignite Remy's temper.

Quinn's exasperated "Micah!" sounded beneath his reply: "Tell him to bring you back."

"I'm not going to sit in that room taking visitors like I'm hosting a wake." Eden's voice was as vehement as it was fractured.

"What kind of car is it? Which direction are you headed?" Micah demanded.

"I'm not kidnapping her," Remy boomed. "If she wants me to leave her by the side of the road, I will, but she got into this car all by herself."

"Remy can drop me at a hotel. I have my wallet. I'm an adult. Don't worry about me," Eden insisted.

"Which hotel?" Quinn asked. "I'll meet you with your things."

"Thank y— Oh." Eden released a small curse as she delved into her purse. "I have your keys." She held them up. "I was going to take your car."

"You pack her bag. I'll meet her," Micah commanded.

"I really think this is a job for a maid of honor," Quinn argued.

"You two work it out. I'll text when I know where I'm staying," Eden muttered and ended the call. She dropped her phone into her purse and set it on the floor, where the incoming calls and texts were muffled by the weight of her skirt. "I swear those two need to have sex and get it over with."

"Is that what you'd like? For me to leave you at a hotel? Because my helicopter is waiting at the heliport near the falls."

"Oh." She frowned with confusion. "Isn't this your car? I thought Hunter said last night that you were driving in from Toronto."

"It is." It was a long story about wanting to

get to the wedding as slowly as possible and away from it as quickly as possible. That's why his pilot had brought his two-rotor Sikorsky, capable of speeds near three hundred miles an hour.

Perhaps it wasn't that long a story. Perhaps it was perfectly obvious what his motives had been.

"I have commitments at home."

"In Martinique?"

"Montreal." Such was the perk of owning homes in many places. He could prevaricate with something close to the truth.

"I need to go home, too," she murmured, sounding as though she was speaking to herself. She turned her face to the window. There was a pang in her voice as she said, "I need to know, though. Was it part of your feud with Micah to set me up for this? To ruin my wedding *and* my company?"

"Wow." Remy tightened his hands on the wheel, reluctant to excavate his thoughts and feelings on the wedding and its train wreck of an outcome, but he damn well wouldn't be accused of sabotaging Bellamy Home and Garden. "Much as I'd like to claim that much superpower, no. I was as shocked as everyone else."

"That's not true." Her head snapped around. "You recognized her."

A hard pulse shot through him. Not guilt. Not quite. But she was right.

"We had drinks with Amelia and her friend last summer. I didn't know it went beyond that between Hunter and her."

"You must have presumed, though. You brought him here to pick up women, didn't you? That's what Vienna implied."

"Is that what Vienna implied? That I arrange hookups for other men? There's a name for that and I'm shocked Vienna used it to describe me. I've always considered us friends."

Eden *tsked* and looked away. "I'm just saying you're the one who brought him here."

"And what's the minimum sentence for that, Your Honor? You and Hunter hadn't been introduced yet. What he and I did last summer had nothing to do with you." Hunter had mentioned Vienna was trying to set him up and Remy had commiserated because his own sister was forever matchmaking, but that was all they'd said on the subject. "You know what Hunter's legal troubles were. I brought him here to golf and drink craft beer. To decompress."

"Is that what the kids call it these days," Eden said with a sniff of disdain.

"Hey, if you want to blame me for your wedding being called off, go ahead. My conscience is clear."

"Is it? You're confident you didn't plant a baby of your own that will pop out of the woodwork any second?"

"That's not where babies come from."

She rolled her eyes and turned her face back to the window.

"And, yes. I'm sure." Remy loved sex and women had been throwing themselves at him from the time he topped five feet. He was now six-two, healthy, rich and rubbed elbows with celebrities. He also knew when a server was flirting because she'd seen his name on his Centurion credit card and was vying for a free trip to the Caribbean. Sex was never a currency for him. He had seen Amelia's friend home, thanked her for a nice evening and hadn't thought about her since.

"Why would you care if I did?" he asked, zeroing in on the most salient point.

"I don't," she assured him, stubbornly keeping her face turned away.

He heard her swallow, though. He smiled with grim satisfaction without letting himself wonder why.

They wound along the Niagara River in silence, rows of grapes flickering on the hillsides above her.

"You never told him," he noted.

"Who? Oh. I told him you and I had met. Once." She began to fiddle with the veil attached to her hair.

"But not about what happened at the club."

"It wasn't relevant."

"You don't think it would be relevant to your fiancé that you nearly got his best friend arrested?"

"You and Micah nearly got yourselves arrested. And Micah has told me repeatedly that your interest in me was *not* personal or sincere, so *my* conscience is clear."

Her veil came free and she pushed it into the back seat, shaking it off her fingers as though it was as sticky as spider silk. She began removing the fernlike pearl-and-sequin doodad from above her ear.

"You really didn't know who I was when you came on to me in Paris?" he asked with skepticism.

"You think *I* came on to *you*?" Her voice rose with outrage. "You were using me to get to Micah!"

"I want less than zero contact with anyone in your family," Remy said, because it was supposed to be true. It had to be.

He geared down with enough aggression to make the Audi's engine growl.

"Then why are you helping me?" she asked with a crack of wildness in her voice.

Why, indeed.

"Because Hunter is my friend," he said with a casual shrug. "He would have quietly called things off if he had known he had a child. A baby is more vulnerable than you are, so his priority shifted to where it needed to go. I'm confident he feels like a sack of dirt, jilting you so publicly. He would want me to help you if I could. He would do the same for me."

"Said another way, your loyalty toward Hunter outweighs your hatred of me and Micah?"

Did he hate her? Remy veered from prodding at that exposed nerve. "Hunter saved my life once. I owe him a favor, no matter how unsavory."

She made a noise that was halfway between being insulted and astonished. "How? Did he suck snake venom from your ankle? Catch a bullet with his teeth?"

"He kept me from freezing to death, if you must know." He rarely mentioned it, still feeling like a callow idiot.

"Really? Where? How?" Her tone had shifted to concerned curiosity.

"U of T. I skipped a year in elementary school so I was younger than the other freshmen. That didn't stop me from trying to keep up at the frat parties." He had lost his parents the year before and his grandfather's health had already been failing. "Hunter found me passed out in the snow. He got me back to my room and stayed while I lost my guts. Then he shared his notes for the two days of classes that I missed."

"But *you* didn't feel a need to tell him you had met *me*," she pointed out. "You waited until he brought it up."

He felt her gaze on the side of his face like a bonfire throwing heat and light.

"I thought about it." His shock on seeing her again, and his libido's quick surge of hunger that had only grown more insatiable in the intervening years, had prompted him to throw up a defensive wall. He had acted as if there had never been anything between them because there never could be. "Hunter hates drama. I didn't want to ruin his court win by publicly dragging his new girlfriend."

"You had other opportunities. The engagement party. The bachelor party. You could have dropped him a text anytime in the last eight months."

"Did you *want* me to tell him?"

"No. I don't know," she muttered, exhaling with frustration.

He waited, but she didn't add anything.

"In my perfect world, I would never cross paths with your brother again," Remy said. "But that wasn't reason enough to get in the way of Hunter's life plan. Whatever this feud is that Micah thinks we're engaged in, he's the only one playing."

"Really. Because that's what he said about you." Her tone was pithy. Her big brown eyes were swallowing her face, swimming in confusion.

"Damn." He almost missed his turn. "Do you want to come with me? I can drop you in Toronto." He pointed at the sign that warned of low-flying helicopter traffic.

"Oh. Yes. Thank you. I would really appreciate that."

He snorted. They were enemies, he reminded himself, and he only wished he felt it more deeply.

Remy drew to a stop outside a heliport where colorful flags hung motionless in the afternoon sun. A family picnicked on a table nearby and a woman pointed at Eden as she emerged from the car.

"Look! They're getting married in a helicopter!"

Not. But Eden didn't want to curdle everyone's ice cream with a glower so she picked up her skirts and followed Remy into the building.

"You're early, sir." A young man straightened from chatting up the pretty young woman behind the heliport's check-in counter. "I had a bird strike on my way in. One of the rotors is damaged…" His voice trailed off with confusion as he noticed Eden behind him.

"It's being repaired?" Remy asked.

"Not yet." The young man dragged his distracted attention back to Remy. "They didn't have a spare here. The replacement is on its way. Their mechanic can install it when it arrives, but I expected you to be three or four hours at least."

"I'll charter one of yours," Remy said to the young woman who had a name tag that read Andrea.

"All of our machines are in the air," Andrea said with an apologetic look. "We're fully booked for tours." She gestured at the family in the waiting area.

A boy was guiding his toy helicopter on a path around the coffee table. His adolescent brother studied Eden with puzzled curiosity. Their mother met Eden's eyes with a stare that both dared and pleaded with her not to disappoint her young family.

It had probably taken her all year to save up for this treat for her boys. Eden was willing to tell her what kind of day she was having, though, to see if they could come to an understanding.

"Let me have a look," Remy said gruffly, shifting his gaze from the family to Eden. He flickered his eyes at the gown that was beginning to weigh on her like a soggy fishing net. "If I can't fix it myself, it's likely to be a few hours. Maybe call your friend to come get you?"

Seriously? He thought she would plant herself in that tiny waiting room eating dry popcorn until Quinn got here?

"Is there somewhere more comfortable where we could wait?" she asked Andrea as Remy walked out to the tarmac.

"We have some partner hotels who are very good to us. Let me make a call."

Eden had meant a private lounge, but Andrea was already dialing and, yes, she would prefer a hotel.

She took a quick peek at her own phone. There were a plethora of texts and voice mails—her mother, Micah, Quinn, Vienna and other guests from the wedding. Oof. Shareholders. BH&G's chief financial officer was also trying to reach her.

This was a seriously terrible, no-good awful day.

"They're trying to get off on their honeymoon, but there's a mechanical issue." Andrea's giggle penetrated Eden's awareness. "No. Not that kind! But they *are* anxious for some alone time." She winked at Eden's stunned expression. "Be a cupid— Oh, wait. Let me ask." She tucked the phone into her neck. "Budget?"

"Money's no object," Eden said flatly. The cost of her wedding was up in flames. What was one more hotel room on top of it?

"The best you have. Perfect," Andrea purred into the phone. "They'll be there shortly." She hung up and scribbled out an address. "Ask for Jorge. Tell them Andrea sent you." She pronounced it *On-dray-yah*.

Eden accepted the chit of paper and wondered if one really could die from a thousand paper cuts, because she was ready to give it a whirl.

Remy strode in from the tarmac with a scowl of annoyance. "It's not something I want to risk. I'll have to wait for the repair."

"No problem. *On-dray-yah* booked us a

room." Eden said it with an admirable lack of sarcasm.

"Great." He took the directions and they went back out to his car.

Eden dropped back into her seat with defeat. Exhaustion was catching up to her. Not only from her poor sleep last night, but also from the marathon that was the organization of a wedding and the fraught emotional journey of taking control of BH&G only to discover it was adrift on stormy seas.

"I kind of want to get drunk off my face," she said as he pulled away from the heliport.

"Fill your boots. I have to fly later so I'll stick to water."

Maybe she should stay the night after all. Quinn would happily get drunk with her.

A few minutes later, Remy pulled into the shaded portico of a ritzy hotel. A man in a hotel uniform hurried out to greet them. His name tag read Jorge.

"You must be Andrea's honeymooners. Let's get you comfortable." He took the duffel from Remy's popped trunk, then looked with puzzlement from Eden to the empty trunk to her parade float of a dress.

"Do you have a boutique in your lobby? Send up a selection," Remy said tersely. "Put everything on my card." He handed it over.

Moments later, they were shown into a top-floor suite.

"It's the only thing that wasn't booked. I hope it suits?" Jorge asked.

It had a full living room with an electric fireplace, a kitchenette, a bedroom with a king-size bed and a Jacuzzi tub with shutters that stood open, allowing the bathers to take in the spectacle of the waterfall beyond the floor-to-ceiling windows.

Eden paused to take in the massive wonder that she had never made the time to see before. It was a stunning sight. Frothy, green-blue water poured over a horseshoe-shaped ridge. Mist billowed off the heavy curtain and floated toward the cloudless sky.

Housekeeping staff were hustling around, setting out a bucket of champagne and gift baskets of fruit and other snacks. One paused to light some candles. Eden shook her head.

"That isn't necessary." Hysteria was threatening to explode out of her. "Can you all please leave?"

"She really is in a hurry," one muttered as they melted away.

The door shut and there was only the faint but distinct rush of water over the falls.

"If you laugh, I will throw myself off that balcony right now," Eden warned Remy.

"I'm not enjoying this, if that's what you're suggesting." He began unbuttoning his morning coat, then halted. His cheek ticked. "Do you need help getting out of that?"

"And wear what?" she cried.

"There must be a robe in the bathroom. Or…" He moved his duffel onto the sofa and dug through it, coming up with a gray T-shirt and maroon shorts with a drawstring.

Dear Lord, those looked so comfortable she could have wept.

"I'm about ready to cut myself free of this," she conceded. It was the foundation layer of shapewear that was killing her. "If you could just open the little catches…" She fiddled at the base of her spine, but the hooks and eyes were hidden behind a fold of satin.

She turned her back and he came up behind her.

"Your skirt is in the way." The satin shifted against her legs as he brushed it aside.

He stepped closer and pressed bunched silk to the backs of her thighs. Her skin tightened. Her scalp tingled with awareness of his looming presence. She thought she felt his breath against the back of her neck, but she was barely breathing herself. Her eyes drifted shut. His light touch grazed where the back dipped to expose the top of her spine.

"They're behind the—"

"Yes, I've worked it out." His voice sounded strange. Deep, but tight. His fingers slid under the edge of the satin, where it hugged the skin of her back. The bodice tightened slightly.

Her nipples stung and a weighted heat rushed into the place between her thighs. A noise like a sob tried to escape her throat.

There was the barest hint of release, then the squeeze again as he drew the gown tight so he could release the next hook.

"It's a pretty gown. It suits you."

"Thanks?" Was he not drowning in sensuality and absurdity, the way she was?

Another constriction, then another release.

"Does that hurt? It left a mark here." His thumb lightly grazed her shoulder blade.

"It's fine." Her voice was pitched three octaves too high.

Slowly, slowly, he freed her. When the front began to slip, she pressed her forearms across it. Her breathing grew more uneven as he worked. Her skin was so sensitive to the brush of his knuckles, she was bereft when the faint contact ceased.

She practically swayed where she stood. This was the part where her groom was supposed to take her to the bed and finish seducing her. *Kiss me. Touch me*, her body cried.

"Thank you," she said, forcing out the words. Her voice was barely a whisper.

She scooped up her purse and started for the bedroom.

"Eden."

Her name in his deep voice halted her.

Her head swam at the conflicting dictates between rational thought and carnal desires. She reeled at his calling her back, unprepared for whatever he was about to ask her.

"Yes?"

"Don't forget these." He offered his shirt and shorts.

She snatched at them. "Thanks."

Mortified, she hurried into the bedroom.

CHAPTER FIVE

REMY WAS SERIOUS about zero alcohol when he had to operate anything larger than a toaster, especially an aircraft, but damn, did he want a drink.

He settled for an icy bottle of spring water and drank it so fast he gave himself a throbbing ache behind his left eye.

Too bad it didn't numb the pulsing heat behind his fly.

Five years ago, the moment he had realized who Eden was, she had become more than off-limits to him. He would call this inconvenient desire *taboo* if it didn't sound so deliberately titillating. The fact that she had just ended her relationship with his best friend made her even more forbidden, but his libido didn't seem to care.

He rubbed his face, trying to erase the jumble of thoughts and emotions flooding into his head. The whole time she'd been involved with

Hunter, he'd been trying to use their relationship to fuel some sort of repulsion in himself, but it had never worked. He hated thinking of her in bed with anyone, but in the grander scheme of things, he really didn't care whom she slept with. Everyone had a history, including him.

Nothing seemed to change how he reacted to her. The only thought in his head as he had stood so close to her while unfastening her dress was that she smelled amazing. Any man would be undone by the graceful line of her spine, appearing inch by inch. It had been all he could do not to dip his head and taste her skin where her neck met her shoulder, especially when he had noted her fine trembles. They had matched the unsteadiness in his hand, as though they were vibrating on the same wavelength.

His eyes drifted closed and he once again saw her smooth, narrow back. The gown's satin against the luster of her skin had mesmerized him. The edges had tickled his knuckles, making him want to draw out undressing her until they were both crazed with lust. He imagined the dress falling loose at the front, inviting his touch to slide around and cup her breast. Her flesh would be warm and weighty, filling his palm, firming the way his flesh was firming—

What the hell was this chemistry between them? Why was it so potent? It had poured into him from that first glimpse he'd had of her in the Louvre and had been simmering and sizzling within him ever since. It was maddening. Nearly irresistible.

He moved to the window, barely taking in the view as he considered whether to walk out on her. He could text Vienna to send Quinn or Micah here. There was no reason he had to stay, even though he had offered to take her to Toronto. *Just make the call.*

A knock at the main door broke into his brooding. As he crossed to open it, he braced himself to dodge a thrown fist, half expecting Micah to have found them.

It was Jorge with a rolling rack of clothing, apologizing profusely for interrupting. "I wasn't sure if I should…" He flicked his gaze around, looking for Eden.

"Thanks." Remy slipped him a tip, took back his credit card and closed the door.

If only he was about to have sex with Eden. If only.

Snap out of it.

He took a cursory look through the options they had delivered, then released a sigh at himself before going to the bedroom door. He knocked and called, "The clothes are here. You don't have to wear mine."

No answer.

Now he was growing aroused thinking of his clothes against her skin.

He would leave, he decided. But he was done with this wedding suit. He peeled off his jacket and tie on his way to where his duffel still sat on the couch. A pair of low-waist trousers in pale green came to hand along with a short-sleeved shirt patterned with asymmetrical shapes in red, yellow, and green on an ocean-blue background.

He was known for his fashion choices, but his flair was by association. His sister had always been enthralled with textures and fabrics. She had begun designing the minute their grandmother had taught her to thread a needle. She worked for a top label in New York and used Remy as a walking mannequin for her creations. He didn't mind. He genuinely liked the colors and cuts she chose for him.

His sister. Thinking of her certainly killed his lingering arousal. She was yet another reason—the core reason—he shouldn't be anywhere near Eden.

He stripped, sighing in relief as the air-conditioned room brought down his temperature.

"Oh! I'm so sorry!" Eden's voice blurted as the door latch clicked open and slammed shut.

Remy swore and snatched up his trousers, keeping his back to the door as he shot his legs into them. As he adjusted himself and zipped, he called, "I'm dressed."

He hurried to thread his arms into the light shirt, hearing the bedroom door slowly reopen behind him.

"I didn't know if you heard me," he said, glancing over his shoulder to see she was wearing a hotel robe.

"I heard the door and honestly thought you left. You don't have to stay. I'm not going to do anything rash." She moved to the rack and began flicking through the sparse selection. She sounded as though she'd been crying.

His heart lurched. He turned to see she was holding a shapeless top in camel-brown against her front. The color leeched any vibrancy from her face. Her makeup was smudged and lines scored both sides of her unhappy mouth.

"You definitely need an intervention if you're considering wearing that," he said as he pulled out a silvery pink skirt and a sleeveless silk turtleneck in buttercup-yellow. "Keep it bright," he suggested as he hooked both across the top of the rack. "Don't let anyone see how much you're hurting."

Her thick black lashes lifted and her dark brown gaze flicked over the loud colors in his own shirt, then rose to meet his eyes. Hers were filled with questions.

"Or so I've been told." He walked away, shoving his hands into his pockets.

"I don't know how to feel," she said heavily. "I'm so angry, I want to punch Hunter in the throat, but the fact that his priorities are in order tells me I wasn't wrong to trust him, just under-informed. I keep telling myself none of this was my fault, but I'm the one who wanted the big wedding. That's why there were so many people there, witness to my disgrace. I'm so nauseous—"

"Are you pregnant?" A thick blade seemed to slice across his chest.

"No." Her eyes went wide with surprise at how intensely he had reacted.

"You're sure?"

"Yes." She shuffled a few more items on the rack, her complexion darkening with a flush.

She paced restlessly away without choosing anything, moving to pull the bottle of sparkling rosé from the bucket. "Maybe tequila would be better." She looked toward the bar and shoved the bottle back into the ice. "I should probably eat something first."

There was a cellophane-wrapped basket on the coffee table. She peered at the butter cookies and mixed nuts on offer, then pressed her hand to her stomach.

"You'd think I'd have an appetite. I've been starving myself for three months. And, yes, I know how unhealthy that is, mentally and physically. Again, I'm the one who wanted this pageant. Hunter told me flat out his preference was something quiet at a courthouse."

"His stepmother." That woman had been making public scenes as long as Remy had known Hunter and Vienna. Well before, from what Hunter had told him.

"He went along with what I wanted and I wanted the fairy tale. As if there is such a thing. I think I was compensating."

"For?"

Eden went back to the pink bubbly. It was from a local winery. She peeled off the foil to reveal a cut-glass stopper. As she struggled to pry it out, Remy started toward her.

She handed him the bottle and walked away.

"I don't really want it. I didn't want any of this. I didn't want to marry him! There. I said it." She dropped onto the sofa and hid her face behind her hands, buckling forward as though in pain. "My life is a disaster and I'm so humiliated I want to die, but I'm relieved."

Remy stared at the bottle in his hand. *Don't do it. You're flying later.*

"You don't love him?" There was a fine rattle in the depths of his chest.

She lifted a culpable face, then said defensively, "He doesn't love me, either. It was an arrangement that had benefits for both of us."

Remy quickly saw how pairing with a name like Bellamy would have fixed a lot of Hunter's PR problems. He didn't know what she would have gained that couldn't have been achieved through the various business mergers they had already announced, though.

For some reason, learning that it had been a marriage of convenience, not real feelings, made him furious. He had accepted Hunter marrying her because his friend had had some terrible blows in life. Hunter deserved to be happy. At heart, he was a decent man, and Remy had known Hunter would treat Eden with care and respect.

But he hadn't loved her? Not even a little?

Was Hunter even *sorry* that he'd treated her so badly today?

There was a loud pop and the stopper flew across the room, hitting the ceiling before it dropped to the carpet.

Eden instinctively covered her head, watching as Remy swooped for a glass. He caught the foam as it began to overflow and offered the flute to her.

Her throat was an arid wasteland, but she waited for him to pour a glass for himself. He only set the open bottle back in the ice.

"Aren't you having any?" she asked.

"I said I'd fly you to Toronto," he reminded her stiffly.

"Right. So I can get back to work." She let out a long, heavy exhale, thinking of the marriage contract she would review. The agreements she and Hunter had signed were contingent on their marriage being finalized, but surely something could be salvaged.

All her problems were supposed to be solved by now! This champagne in her hand ought to be a celebratory toast for saving the family legacy. Of winning.

The bubbles stung her nose and the alcohol was sour on her tongue.

"You're going back to work?" Remy had found the stopper and moved to plug the neck of the bottle. "I would have thought you had time booked for a honeymoon. Can't you use it to regroup?"

"That's what I resent the most right now! I'm not getting the honeymoon I was promised." She'd been pushing herself like mad, her vacation time the carrot at the end of the stick.

Now she would have to work harder than ever not to lose everything.

Remy had gone very still.

Her words hit her ears.

"I mean swimming and reading." She gulped down another mouthful of cold, sizzling wine. "In Greece. I'm not hitting on you again, if that's what you think. I didn't in the first place. I'm babbling because I'm nervous. Leave if you want to. I'll phone Quinn to come get drunk with me and restart my life in the morning." With a giant hangover, but so what?

He cocked his head. "Why are you nervous?"

Because he put her on her back foot with questions like *Why are you nervous?*

"It's not the most comfortable thing to be trapped with someone who hates me."

"I don't *hate* you." His stoic expression didn't quite disguise the flash of forceful reaction behind it. "That is the issue, Eden. I should hate you. Or at least want nothing to do with you. It's not that easy. It never has been," he muttered and moved to the window, showing her only his rigid back.

She sagged, but not with relief. Not when she was nursing anxiety that this could be some ploy he had decided to enact.

"Can I ask you something? Will you please be honest with me this time?" she asked.

"I didn't know who you were," he said starkly, guessing what she was going to say. "I know why Micah thinks I was trying to use you. Our families have history. I don't want to get into that, but what happened at the night-club, when we kissed—that was basic, mutual attraction." He turned his head to pin her with the golden spike of his gaze. "It *was* mutual, wasn't it?"

"Yes." She took another sip to dampen her whisper-dry throat.

"But nothing can come of it, Eden. That's why I didn't interfere between you and Hunter. I'll see you home because it's the decent thing to do, but that's all this is."

"Then we'll never see each other again?" She didn't hear the pang in her voice so much as feel it as it felt like a shard of glass lodged in her chest. At least when she was marrying his best friend, she had thought she might run in to Remy now and again. She had known she would hear about him through Hunter and know he was well.

Why did that matter so much to her?

She realized he hadn't answered her. He stood so still, so very still.

Her pulse throbbed unevenly in her throat as

she replayed her own words in her head. *We'll never see each other again.* A rushing sound filled her ears.

"Remy?" She could hardly speak. "Am I deluding myself? Is it just me?"

"Eden." Her name was an imprecation. He dug the heels of his hands into his eyes. "Don't do this to me."

"Don't what? Don't tell you how I feel? Don't be *honest*? Why not? What do I have left to lose?"

"You have nothing to *gain*." He swung his head around and his flashing gaze warned her to stay silent.

Even so, the words left her.

"I think about you all the time. I always have." They didn't come out in a burst, but in a soft, faltering trickle. The emotions behind them were a river, though, one that brimmed its banks and flooded the room, soaking everything with her truth. "This is the first time you've properly spoken to me since Paris. If you had said something before today, I wouldn't have let the wedding get this far—"

"Damn it, *stop*. You want honesty?" He rounded on her, but his voice was fatalistic. "I want you, Eden. It sits inside me like a black hole that swallows up everything else. It eats at me so I feel empty all the time. *Hun-*

gry." He set his fist against his diaphragm. "It hurts. I wanted to kill him for marrying you and now I want to kill him for scorning you. *This is hell."*

She covered her mouth, pressed back into the sofa by his vehemence. By his suffering.

"But it can't happen. Accept it. I have."

"It's just us here." The words slipped out of her, impetuous. Desperate.

A distant part of her urged her to show some sense. She knew Micah would never forgive her for so much as getting in Remy's car, but they had had something in Paris. It had been interrupted and the not knowing what could have been had left her with an ache of yearning that had stalled her in some way. If she couldn't have Remy then it didn't matter whom she married. All men were the same because they weren't him.

"No one would know," she added.

"Damn you, Eden!" He walked past her, snatching up his duffel on his way to the door.

"Remy!" She shot to her feet and cried his name exactly as if he was striding off the balcony and into Niagara Falls.

He stopped and stood there for one, two… three beats.

He dropped his bag and his hand shot out to slam the inner latch across the door so it couldn't be opened from the outside. He turned.

"I *don't* pick up women. Some of my relationships have been shorter than others, but I have relationships, Eden. I can't have one with you, though. Do you understand that? This would only be today. An hour. We couldn't tell anyone. Ever. If Hunter found out—"

"If Micah found out," she said with a catch in her voice. "I don't care about any of that. I really don't."

"After this, it goes back to the way it was, like we didn't even know one another. Is that really what you want?" His face twisted with conflict.

"No," she confessed with a chasm opening in her chest. "But I'll take it."

He closed his eyes, swearing as he fell back against the door with a defeated thump.

"Come here, then."

Eden ran across and he stepped forward to catch her. She was off her bare feet, secure in arms she hadn't known long enough to miss, but she had. When his mouth landed on hers, she was *home*.

Bright sunshine filled her, searing away her skin from the inside out so all she felt was him. His mouth drank at hers as though he was parched beyond reason. They were both wild and greedy and *joyous*. It was such a brilliantly perfect kiss, her eyes stung with emotion.

"Tell me you're sure," he said in a gravelly voice.

"I'm sure. Don't stop." She touched his jaw, steering his mouth back to hers.

How could a mouth, a pair of lips, be so firm yet so soft? So demanding, yet so giving? She reveled in the way he kissed her, as though she meant everything to him. This was what she had longed for the most. This feeling like she was *The One*.

In the same way that he was *The One*.

A thumping, terrifying urgency stalked around her as she clung to him, but she ignored it, letting herself sink into this moment. She memorized the feel of his strong shoulders beneath her palms and the soft abrasion of stubble coming in on his chin. His hands slid across her back, petting and massaging and pressing her into him, as though he wanted her impression to remain against his front forever.

She wriggled and stood on her toes, trying to get closer still. Her robe loosened and her thighs felt the rough fabric of his trousers.

He kept saying her name—"Eden, Eden"—as though he couldn't believe she was real. His mouth went down her neck and she flicked her tongue against his earlobe. His breath hissed and she smiled.

Then his hand slid between them and tugged at her belt, pulling it completely free. He drew back and watched her reaction as he let her robe fall open.

She didn't flinch with shyness. She probably should have. She wore only a slash of bronze lace across her hips, no bra, but she had been his all this time, if only he had noticed. If only he had grown solemn and his chest had shaken, while his reverent gaze slid down.

His hand rested on her bare hip while his thumb traced the edge of lace. It was barely a caress, but her stomach sucked in and she grew light-headed. A flicker of satisfaction touched the corner of his mouth.

She brought up her hands to begin releasing the buttons on his shirt, one by one.

He didn't move, letting her do it in her time. He held her gaze and the only sound was their uneven breathing and the muted thunder of the falls outside.

When she spread his shirt and splayed her hands across his firm abs, his breath rattled. He cupped the back of her neck and drew her in for a new kiss, one that was hot and slow and made her toes curl. Her bare breasts met the hot surface of his chest and such a hard jolt of pleasure went through her, she sobbed with delight.

His smile flashed once, then his eyelids grew heavy with need. He kissed her again, deeper, sliding his tongue against her bottom lip and into her mouth. Her knees shook and the rest of her went limp.

She wrapped her arms around his waist, stroking his back and learning the landscape of his spine and shoulder blades and the shape of his backside through his trousers.

It struck her how natural this felt, considering she'd never been this naked with anyone before. She nuzzled her face into the crook of his neck and let her body tell him how much she enjoyed the roaming of his hands beneath the robe, how much she craved more. So much more.

He cradled one of her breasts and slid his lips down the front of one shoulder, halting with his hot breath bathing the swell. He swore softly. "I don't have a condom."

"There's some in the bedroom." Andrea had stoked the impression of newlyweds in a hurry to consummate their nuptials. The hotel had delivered.

Eden stepped back and folded her robe closed, then took his hand, leading him to the basket beside the bed. Erotic ideas had filled her imagination when she had glimpsed the candles, massage oil, ruffle-edged blindfold, lubricant and condoms.

"They're ultrathin," she pointed out, trying to keep a straight face through her bemusement. "And vegan."

"And gluten-free, I hope?" He tilted the basket. "No handcuffs? It's our *honeymoon*."

They both chuckled unevenly. Hers held an edge of helpless, hopeless sadness that this wasn't such a thing at all.

"The energy drinks are," she pointed out. "Gluten-free. Gotta stay hydrated."

She leaned into him. He hugged her, but his expression sobered.

"Don't ask me again if I'm sure," she chided. "I am. Aren't you?"

His next laugh was a rough exhale that held little humor and a lot of frustrated desire. "I want this so much it terrifies me."

She smiled, but it didn't stick. She turned her face into his bare shoulder and kissed the hollow there, then lifted her mouth, yearning for his.

With a groan he dragged her against his front. They sank back into the delicious pool of passion.

Her sense of rightness expanded. It was odd

how sure she was, given she didn't know him that well. There was a tiny concern still hovering that he might be using her, but in this moment, she didn't care if he was. He had been haunting her fantasies for years. If circumstances had been different, she had no doubt he would have been her first lover.

If she had had that affair in her history, she might not have felt so boxed in by her impending marriage. At least this way, she rationalized, she would have the memory of the growling sound he made as she slid her hands up his sides and around to his back while she brushed her breasts against his chest.

"Why do you smell so good?" His breath played across her shoulder before he dipped and stole a hot damp taste of her nipple. "Like cloves and…"

Whatever he said was lost as he enclosed the tip of her breast and a moan of luxury rolled up from deep in her throat. The way he drew on her sent shots of heat fluttering through her belly and pulsing between her legs. She felt drunk on her own sensuality.

She was so hot! She let the robe fall off her shoulders and he made a sound of gratification, straightening to drop his shirt. His eyes were molten gold as he shed his pants. His gaze was so bright, so illuminated by lust, it was hard to hold his stare, but she couldn't look away. The throbbing between her thighs intensified.

"Tell me what you like." His fingertip traced the edge of lace beneath her navel then followed the seam at her hip. Slowly, slowly, he followed her bikini line, filling her sex with a heavy ache and a sensation of empty longing.

He watched his own caress with narrow-eyed intensity, voice deepening to a gruff, animalistic sound. "I want you so satisfied that I ruin you for anyone else."

A catch of helpless laughter left her. He already had.

His mouth twisted with self-deprecation. "I don't know when I became such a Neanderthal. Somewhere between the living room and here."

He was still tickling at her bikini line, but now he brushed a light fingertip across the front of bronze lace, teasing the plump flesh beneath.

"I want to taste you here. Take them off?"

"You can. If you want to." Her cheeks grew hot and her voice was a husk of itself. Her inhibition seemed to have equally eroded. She was shaking and barely able to stand, but she held very still as he eased down her panties to let them fall at her ankles.

His nostrils flared and he took her hand, helping her step out of them, then he brought her hand to his mouth and kissed her fingertips, moving to the underside of her wrist and the inside of her elbow. He kissed her collarbone and the point of her chin, and his teeth scraped her earlobe.

"Lie back," he urged.

She melted onto the bed and he followed. His hot weight blanketed her as he kept up those hypnotizing kisses. Each one was tender and inciting, making her soft and tense at once. She relaxed, but she wanted more. She needed more.

"Remy."

"Not yet, *ma chérie*. I want to taste all of you." He rolled her onto her stomach and continued brushing his damp mouth across her skin, tongue dabbing at her spine and into the hollow of her lower back. "You have dimples here, too," he noted, kissing the top of each cheek.

His lips touched the backs of her thighs, the backs of her knees…

"Remy, please." She rolled to face him and he ran his hand from her knee to her thigh, squeezing her quadriceps.

"I only have this once," he said gruffly. "Let me do it right."

A jagged strike of lightning went into her heart. He leaned to press a kiss to her stomach, then shifted between her legs, easing one of her thighs over his shoulder.

Her scalp tightened. Here again, she should have been more self-conscious, but he was so reverent, so confident and so unhurried.

"Oh," she groaned as he slowly tasted her, deepening his caress in increments, working zings of pleasure from her center outward, nurturing them into stronger and stronger pangs of delight. She writhed in pleasure, lost to the earthy joy of it.

She was tempted, oh-so tempted, to let him take her over the edge like this. She was shaking, edging close to climax, but she wanted that other intimacy. The thing she'd been dreaming of for five long years.

"Remy, please," she moaned. "I want you inside me."

"I want that, too," he growled. He shed his underwear, then stood on his knees over her as he applied a condom.

He was very good at it, for a man who didn't make a habit of hooking up.

"Maybe, um, a little of the lubricant?" she

suggested, suddenly nervous as she realized this might hurt. "It's not flavored, is it?"

"No." He anointed himself, then caressed between her legs with his slick finger, making her bite her lip as desire rushed back to a level of near combustion. "You have no idea how many times I've thought about this."

She shook, fighting not to climax, and held up her arms.

He loomed over her, bracing on his elbow. She bent her legs, catching her lip with her teeth as he guided himself into position.

It struck her that this was how many a bride felt on her wedding night. Eager and apprehensive. Aroused, but feeling a little awkward at how brazen this act was.

"Second thoughts?" he asked, flashing his eyes at her, perhaps sensing her tension. "We can stop."

"I don't want to stop. I'm wishing I was good enough at this to ruin *you* for anyone else." Her eyes stung. Her throat and chest heated at how true that was.

"What makes you think you won't?" His face tightened as he shifted slightly. His flesh prodded for entry.

She made herself relax, but her hands tightened on his shoulders.

"Does it hurt?" he asked, perplexed.

"No." *A little. Maybe more than a little.* "I'm nervous. Oh." There was a startlingly real sensation as his thick shape forged into her. The stretch stung quite a lot. She bit her lip again.

He froze. "This is hurting. I'll stop."

"No, I *want* this. Please keep going." She touched his back, urging him.

He pressed a little more insistently, watching her with concern.

The sensation was remarkable. So intimate, she blushed. So intense, she trembled. It hurt, but she experienced a silly rush of pride as she took him in. He filled her so deeply, his pulse seemed to beat within her. The sensation of being joined with him in such an indelible way brought bright tears to her eyes.

"Eden," he said through gritted teeth.

"It's okay. The hurt is fading. I like how it feels."

Myriad emotions flickered across his expression. "Damn it. Are you a virgin?"

"Are you mad?" she asked with apprehension.

"I'm—" He was braced on his elbows and hung his head so his scorched laugh of disbelief huffed against her chin. "Why would you do this? Make your first time *me*?"

He lifted his head and searched her gaze

for answers. There were a thousand facets in the hammered gold of his eyes. Astonishment and suspicion, exasperation and tenderness, and such humbleness that he made her mouth quiver.

"Do you really have to ask?" she whispered.

He closed his eyes. "No. No, I don't." He cupped her cheek and set a very gentle kiss on her lips. "Don't let me hurt you."

Irony tickled at the corner of her mouth. He would hurt her. Maybe even devastate her. It was inevitable, given the deal they had struck to arrive at this point. He wouldn't hurt her physically, no more than the discomfort she had just suffered. She could tell he was remorseful about that. He was treating her as though she was made from eggshells, holding himself so carefully within her and kissing her so softly that it was a tiny bit frustrating.

In an hour or a day, however, he would turn his back and pretend they had never done this. That would crush her far worse than being publicly thrown over had.

At least they were together right now. She could provoke his rumbling purrlike growl as she stroked the back of his neck and ran her hands down his back. Her tickling exploration across his buttocks provoked a slight thrust of his hips, causing pressure against her most sensitive places, teasing her back to the intense arousal that had made her beg to have him inside her.

She instinctually widened her thighs and rubbed them on his hips, riding them up to his waist. Another shimmer of joyous sensations followed.

Now the noise he made was hedonistic and possessive. He gathered himself as he withdrew slightly and returned.

"Oh," she breathed, so dazzled by pleasure, he seemed to exist in a halo of dancing lights. "I didn't know it would feel like this."

"Me, either," he said gravely, drawing out his next withdrawal and thrust, making them both shudder under the power of it.

Eden lost herself to their lovemaking then, allowing the sheer cataclysmic pleasure of flesh moving within flesh to consume her. Nothing about it felt awkward anymore. It was like the most graceful dance, the most natural union. There was no tracking who caressed and who moaned, who kissed and who caught a sharp breath.

She could have lived forever in this wondrous place, but they were mere mortals who could only withstand so much. As the intensity redoubled on itself, the pleasure heightened to such levels it was excessive. She quivered on the edge of climax.

"Let go." His voice was a rasp of command and plea and exaltation. "I'll come with you." He thrust once more and golden light engulfed her.

CHAPTER SIX

ON HIS FINAL THRUST, Remy experienced a release unlike any other. It took all his control to keep from bruising her with his grip on her shoulder as molten heat and shivering silk and intense pleasure consumed him. It was so good, he nearly blacked out. His blood and nerves and bones were infused with sweet, sharp possessiveness and deep gratitude that this had happened. *Mine. Finally.*

Yet not. Even as his shaking frame sank weakly upon her, his haze of satisfaction was disturbed by… He couldn't call it remorse. Regret? Yes, but not because they were making love. Nothing about this felt wrong. No, he already regretted it could be only this. Once.

And it was over.

His heart was still trying to steady itself as he gathered his strength to lift his weight and withdraw from her. It had to happen, but the act was akin to stepping out of his own skin.

His muscles were shaking, his body still damp with their combined perspiration. Everything in him resisted leaving paradise.

She drew in a startled breath as his relaxed erection slipped f—

He swore bluntly at the rush of cool air on his damp flesh.

"What's wrong?" Her hands dropped from his shoulders and her body went stiff with wariness.

"The condom broke." Why had he trusted freaking novelty skins with Honeymoon Helper stamped on the foil?

"Really?"

"Yes, really. Are you using anything?"

Her pupils seemed to explode, turning her dark brown eyes into inky black pools.

"Birth control? No. We were pl-planning to start a family right away." Her voice faded into a mumble.

Because she was supposed to be doing this with Hunter. His best friend. On their wedding night.

Remy found another handful of sharp curses and thrust himself from the bed.

In the bathroom, he discarded the split latex and splashed cold water onto his face, trying to soak some rational thought back into his head, but it was impossible. Not when there was a new, even more disastrous mess in front of him.

He wanted to crack his head against that idiot in his reflection. *What the hell were you thinking?*

He hadn't been, obviously.

"Remy? Could I, um, have the bathroom?" The quaver in her voice wrung a fresh wince out of him. She was new to this and he was behaving like—

He didn't know how to behave!

"Of course." He went back to the bedroom.

She was standing uneasily in the middle of the room clutching a pillow in front of her to hide her nudity. Maybe for reassurance. She had her thighs pressed tightly together and wore an expression of distress. Her eyes were smudged and smoky. Her hair was fraying out of its conchlike style and was curling behind her ears. The puffiness in her lips and the sleepy sensuality in her eyelids were erotic as hell.

All he wanted to do was drag her back onto the bed they'd wrecked, but she brushed by him and muttered, "Thank you." She threw the pillow on the floor as she closed herself into the bathroom.

He pinched the bridge of his nose and blew out a pained breath.

When he heard the shower come on, he took a step toward the door, wanting to ask if she was okay. Was she hurt? Upset?

Of course, she was upset. *He* had been turned inside out by this development.

With a final, jaded curse, he dressed, then he straightened the bed and left the clothes he'd picked out for her on the foot of it. He spared a moment to examine the condoms. They were within their use-by date and were actually made by a reputable manufacturer. Maybe it had been the wrong type of lubricant?

Did it matter? The condom had broken. That couldn't be reversed.

He went back to the living room and downed the wine that Eden had only tasted. It had gone flat and warm, but his need for a drink had overshot all his other concerns.

He checked in with his pilot, who reported that the repair part should arrive any minute.

I'll need you to fly us to Toronto, Remy texted as he refilled his glass. Text Alister to send someone for my car. Alister was his personal assistant.

The hotel would have to shuttle them to the heliport when the helicopter was ready, but so be it. Remy took another gulp of wine. At least it was cold this time.

He was thinking about opening something

stronger when Eden reappeared. Her face had been washed clean. Her hair was tidied smooth, but still in its arrangement. The bright colors of the skirt and top suited her, making her look more confident and put-together, countering the wary vulnerability in her eyes.

"What happened to not drinking?" she asked as she noted the glass he held.

"My pilot was supposed to drive my car back to Montreal. I asked him to fly us. Someone else will pick it up." He topped up her glass so it wore a fresh head of bubbles.

Her mouth… Damn, she had a pretty mouth, especially when she pouted it that way.

"I've never needed one of those morning-after pills, but I think I can get one over the counter at a pharmacy. I texted Quinn that I would leave her key with the concierge. When she gets here, she can take me."

His heart lurched. "*I* can take you to a pharmacy. Is that what you want?"

"For Quinn to take me?"

"To prevent a pregnancy?"

"It's what you want." The dignity in her voice fractured.

He held his glass so hard it might have shattered in his fist.

"What makes you think that?" he asked.

"Wasn't that the point of the condom? To prevent a pregnancy? You're obviously horrified that it broke. You're pouring me alcohol—"

"Forget that." He snatched up the glass he'd poured and dumped the liquid into the bar sink. "I wasn't thinking." It was time he *started* thinking. He poured out his own. "I'm not *horrified*. I'm—" Seeing a reason to keep seeing her. That's what whispered at him like a devil on his shoulder. "I don't know how to react. This is a lot to process."

"It is." She sank onto the couch, hands in her lap, sightless gaze pinning itself to the middle of the floor.

She looked very young in that moment. Like the nineteen-year-old innocent he had met in Paris, the one who had looked at him with such bewilderment as her brother dragged her from the club.

Into the silence, her stomach growled.

With a pained sob, she set her hand across it and glanced at the abundant baskets of snacks.

"Let's eat. We'll think better." Remy started breaking into them, setting out rustic crackers on the dining table with spreadable cheese, tiny gerkins, stuffed olives and hummus. "Would you rather have room service?"

"No. This is fine." She collected plates and cutlery on her way to the table.

They sat and wordlessly devoured the snacks.

"I think we worked up an appetite," he said wryly as he reached for another handful of deluxe trail mix. "Do you feel better?"

"Yes, but now I want to bust into the one with chocolate."

He rose and brought it to the table. As an afterthought, he opened the door to the Juliet balcony so the sound of the falls and the mist-infused breeze floated in, then sat down again.

"This is actually really romantic," she murmured, wistfully staring at the falls. The corners of her mouth went down.

He knew what she was thinking. *If only this were real.*

"Eden—" He hesitated, but she needed to hear it. He needed to *say* it. "That was the best sex of my life."

An infinite number of emotions flickered across her expression. Amazement at his blunt honesty, shy pleasure at the compliment and profound self-consciousness that he would reference it so openly. Tremulous hope followed with something so naked, it stopped his heart. Then a shadow of anxiety as she remembered the consequences they might face. Finally, her mouth quirked with self-deprecation.

"Me, too," she said huskily.

He snorted. But, yeah. It still didn't compute that she had been a virgin.

"How…?" She was twenty-four. Twenty-five? Peer pressure tended to push people into sex long before now. "You and Hunter were engaged." His friend might not be a serial womanizer, but Hunter had had affairs. Amelia, for instance.

"He was okay with waiting. So was I." Eden set down the dark chocolate truffle she had bitten in half and wiped her fingertips on her napkin. "Before him, I didn't date very seriously. I was busy with school and working with Dad. Also, Micah had convinced me that you had used me in Paris. It messed with my faith in my own judgment where men were concerned— Why are you mad?" She sat back.

Remy tried and failed to erase the flare of temper from his expression.

"The fact your brother thinks I would use a woman for *any reason* says more about him than it does about me. You realize that? Paris had nothing to do with y—"

"Oh, my *gawd*," she cried, throwing herself to her feet so fast her chair toppled. "If I hear one more time that Paris had nothing to do with me… No matter what you were fighting about, I was still in the middle of it! One second we were kissing, the next, you two were at each other's throats. You two *put* me in the middle of it. And it's the reason you and I can't…" She waved between them, face flexing with anguish. "You're in a cold sweat over a broken condom. Because you might become a father? Or because *I* might be your baby's mother?"

Her anger crashed against his own, but it allowed him to compress his simmering antipathy back into the box where he kept it.

"It's me. Isn't it?" she demanded with a tap of one fingernail on the table. "Because Micah is my brother. Say it."

Because Micah was Yasmine's brother. That was the shocking truth of it, but Remy had sworn to his father that he would keep that fact hidden. Forever.

"Given the history between my family and Micah's, yes. You and I are impossible."

"Why?" she cried. "Because of industrial espionage twenty years ago? That's why you're making me take a pill instead of—"

"I'm not making you take that pill!" he interrupted vehemently, also flinging himself to his feet. "If you—" Such conflict gripped him, he could hardly breathe. "Whether you take a pill or not is entirely your decision." He grappled for control of his voice. Of his composure. He was pro-choice all the way. "I'll support you no matter what happens. I'm not afraid to become a father. I always expected I would be one. Eventually."

"But not with me," she choked out with agony.

He moved to grip the rail on the balcony. Maybe he'd been holding out for her, which didn't make any sense whatsoever. He spun back into the room and closed the door.

"What do you want, Eden?" he asked as calmly and rationally as he was able to. "Forget all the rest."

"You haven't told me the rest!"

"Indulge me," he pressed. "Forget Hunter and Micah and even me. Ultimately, this comes down to whether or not you want to take a chance on being pregnant right now. On carrying a baby and delivering it."

Her mouth trembled. Her eyes glossed with emotion. "It's more complicated than that."

"Not really," he chided softly. "Everyone thinks there's a perfect time or circumstance to start a family. We all want to believe we're in control of our lives, but hell, look at Hunter. Life happens. Literally. Plans have to be adjusted."

"And you would adjust yours to accommodate me?" she scoffed. "Maybe nothing will happen. Maybe this entire conversation is moot."

"Maybe," he agreed. "What is the timing like?"

"My cycle?" She gripped her elbows. "I've always been a little irregular when I'm stressed. It's been a really difficult year. I know I don't want to have a baby by someone who resents me for it."

"With," he clarified. "Not *by*, *with* me. I would never blame you for getting pregnant. There were two of us in that bed. If a baby comes along, it's ours."

"Meaning you would want to be involved. See? That means I'm making a decision for both of us."

"No. If you let nature take its course and a pregnancy happens then, yes, I'll be right there with you, every step of the way. But you're the one who has to carry that pregnancy. Right now, *you* have to decide what's right for your body and whether pregnancy is a chance you want to take."

She shook her head. "You can't mean that. What if I decide to take the pill? Then what?" she challenged.

He'd be disappointed as hell, but… "I'll respect whatever choice you make, I swear."

"No pressure." Eden paced toward the window, but didn't take in the view. Her attention was turned inward, her body still simmering with sensuality from their lovemaking.

In that heated tussle, everything in her world had been utterly perfect. She could have existed in the aftermath of twilight joy forever, but he had sworn and pulled away, reacting with such fury, she had been flattened by rejection. And fear, as she realized what a precarious situation she was in.

I'll just take a pill had been her panicked thought in the shower. It was the great undo button, wasn't it?

It was also an action that couldn't be undone, but she had been certain that was what Remy wanted her to do.

Instead, he was saying it was up to her. That was a huge responsibility to carry! What if she did get pregnant? Micah would be furious. Hunter would be…well, who cared if Hunter had to weather another storm of unflattering publicity? Remy was the one who would be affected the most.

She bit her thumbnail, trying not to be swayed by his promise to be with her all the way. What if he was lying? What if this was exactly what Micah had warned her about?

It wouldn't matter, she realized with illogical clarity. She would want the baby regardless. She had always wanted a family. The family she had grown up in had been fractured by her mother's difficult relationship with Micah's father, forcing her only sibling to grow up away from her. When her cousins had started having their children, she had said goodbye to beloved grandparents, then her father. She had never imagined motherhood would be easy, but she had always known she wanted to have a child.

Remy was right about there being no real control on timing, either. Her life was a mess, so today wasn't optimal, but even if she lost the company, she was a very privileged person. She had enough resources that she could afford to support her child.

Most importantly, she didn't know when she would find another man with whom she would want to make love, let alone make a baby. As first times went, Remy had made hers as near to perfect as it could be. She would have no regrets on how conception had happened.

If it happened. Her heart pounded with a mixture of anticipation and trepidation. What if it did? She would be bound to him for a lifetime. Was she ready to take that risk?

She turned to face him and knew she was. Why? Yes, he was handsome and so well-dressed it was blinding, but she wasn't that superficial. She had only interacted with him a few times so she couldn't claim to really know him, but… Was she delusional? She felt as though she knew him at a soul-deep level, even though she couldn't say what he ate for breakfast or whether he preferred cats to dogs.

She trusted him, though. Instinctually. She had climbed into his car in her moment of need because she felt safe with him. She wanted to *be* with him. Her entire being yearned for it, and had since the moment she had met him in Paris.

"I want to see what happens." What if he thought she was trying to trap him?

He paused in tidying up the remnants of their picnic.

"Okay." He nodded gravely. Then he continued using economical movements to close jars and stack the dirty dishes in the sink.

"Really? You're not going to react more strongly than that?" Reveal delight or dismay?

"I'm impatient to know whether it happens, obviously." His mouth twisted with self-deprecation. "But that will take a couple of weeks?" His whiskey-gold eyes fixed on her.

She nodded jerkily. "I think the early tests only work if you to know when you ovulated. I'm not sure, so…"

"So we wait."

She searched his expression because his equanimity didn't make sense.

"Are you *sure* you won't be angry if…?" *If I carry your child?* "You don't want a baby with me, Remy. I know you don't."

His cheek ticked and he turned away, veering from the open bottle of wine to the bar. He unceremoniously snapped the seal on a bottle of whiskey, twisting off the cap as though he was wringing someone's neck.

"It's not ideal," he said, tone so ironic she knew it to be a gross understatement.

She came to the other side of the bar and gripped it.

"Because of Micah. He said your father stole proprietary information from his."

Remy's reaction was to pour a healthy measure of amber liquid into a glass. Then he topped it with the smallest splash of sparkling water from the refrigerator. He offered her the rest of the water.

After the salty snacks, she was dying of thirst. Plus, her mouth was positively arid. She took the glass he offered and poured it out for herself.

"Your brother seems to think I have it in for him. The truth is, I don't think about him at all. If our paths never crossed again, I'd be thrilled."

Her hand unconsciously went to her midriff while a searing pain pinned itself through her chest. Her throat flexed, refusing to swallow the water in her mouth.

Remy had his back to her, so he didn't see her reaction, but now he turned.

"He seems to think my lust for you is retaliation." His matter-of-fact tone caused a flood of pained heat to rise in her cheeks.

Lust? That's all it was?

"The conflict should have remained between our fathers." His cheek ticked with tension. "Micah's father, Kelvin Gould, literally pulled me into it."

"Micah said something once, but he didn't want to get into it. You met his father? Where? When?" And how? Eden had never met Kelvin Gould herself. Micah's father had mostly stayed in Europe, only visiting Canada once that she knew of. Her mother had left her with Grammy Bellamy, her father's mother, while he was in town. Kelvin had developed dementia when Micah was in his late teens and died a few years later.

"It was a middle-school basketball tournament in Toronto."

"When Micah lived with us." She recalled Micah saying that, too. "You would have been eleven? Twelve? I was really young, myself. Not even in school. All I really remember is that Micah was supposed to stay with us, but he went back to boarding school. I cried for weeks and begged to be sent to boarding school when it was time for kindergarten. I thought it meant I would see him there."

"Cute," he said with a dry snort that she took as patronizing.

"I love my brother, Remy."

"I don't doubt it. Or that he loves you." He sipped his drink, gaze fixed on her.

"But," she prompted. "What happened at the game to get him sent back to boarding school?"

"I don't know why he had to leave town. It wasn't that big a deal." He came out from behind the bar and wandered to the window. "The game was much like any other at that age, clumsy and loud. There was a father on the other team's side who was riding his son pretty hard, but I didn't pay much attention. My father noticed, though. He was an assistant coach and chaperoned the away games. I'll never forget the look on his face when he glanced across and recognized Kelvin Gould. It was worse than seeing a ghost. It was a type of hatred that…" Remy swallowed some of his whiskey and there was a rasp in his voice from the alcohol when he continued. "It was murderous. My father was a very generous and loving man. I didn't know he was capable of that sort of lethal revulsion."

A chill settled into her chest. "What happened? Did he confront him?"

"Not immediately. He told me later that he wished he had pulled me from the game the moment he saw Gould. That we had waited on the bus, but I was playing well, having fun. Then Gould saw my father. He figured out which kid was his and started calling out some truly vile things at me. Racist remarks, which was hurtful enough, but I could tell he was doing it because he knew that going after someone he loved was the most effective way to hurt my father. I couldn't stand it. I tripped Micah."

"You said this feud wasn't between you two!"

"I tripped him in a game, Eden. We were kids. The only real damage was to his adolescent pride. But his father left the bleachers and came after me like a street fighter."

"Oh, my God." She touched her cold fingers to her lips.

"Next thing I know, I was waking up on the floor. Dad was over me. One eye was bloodshot and his lip was split. Gould had been removed and Micah was gone, too. My father took me to get checked at the hospital and I never saw

Kelvin Gould again. I didn't see Micah until that night in Paris, when he seemed to think I was continuing what we'd started that day by making advances on you. I'm not that childish," he said derisively.

"He said you were mad that he bought a vineyard, one your family wanted. And that you never let his company bid on your projects."

"That's business," he said, dismissing her suggestion with a flick of his hand. "For the projects we've had, hiring Gould Automation would be like asking a neurosurgeon to give us a haircut."

"So it all goes back to Micah's father thinking yours robbed him?"

"My parents were the ones who were robbed," he said forcefully. "Have you ever looked it up online?"

"I didn't find much." Basically, the story was exactly as Micah had related it. Remy's father had *allegedly* double-crossed his employer by selling proprietary information.

"The story you read was written by the side with the greater financial resources." Remy's spine was rigid. "My parents weren't poor, but they weren't on Gould's level. My father was born in Martinique, and my mother was Haitian. They met while schooling in France and both had family there so it made sense to marry and settle in Paris. My father took a position with Gould Automation as a robotics engineer. He was very talented."

Eden had no doubt. Micah had inherited the conglomerate that helped factories around the world become more efficient. The company had always been well regarded as innovative and profitable.

"The undisputed facts are that my father was a lead engineer working on a project in the Netherlands. His laptop and backup diskettes went missing from their home. Shortly thereafter, a Gould competitor poached the client and built them a system very much like the one my father had been designing."

"Was the competitor ever questioned?"

"They claim it arrived anonymously. Investigations proved nothing except that my father didn't benefit financially. Even so, Kelvin Gould did everything he could to discredit and ruin him. The accusations followed him to Canada. Fortunately, Mom had family in Montreal who were trying to expand from selling package tours to the Caribbean into operating a dedicated fleet of airplanes. My father became a pilot and it all worked out."

Remy was still at the window, keeping his

back to her, which gave her a vague suspicion he wasn't telling her everything.

"So Micah's father attacked you because he believed your father had stolen from him and got away with it? Then, years after that, Micah thought you were still nursing a grudge about his father's attack and came after me? I'm sorry, Remy, but it sounds like you two need to sit down and clear the air. It's not worth holding on to so much acrimony, is it?"

"Not to you. Or Micah. His father's company lost a hundred thousand euros, which is no small sum, I'll grant you, but my family was impacted far more personally and profoundly." He threw back the last of his drink. "So, no thank you. I do not want to kiss and make up with him."

She considered how his parents must have felt—uprooted. Their reputations were shredded and their careers stopped in their tracks. Did Micah think Remy was still covering up for his father? Why did he continue to be so suspicious of him?

The room phone jangled, startling her from her ruminations.

Remy frowned.

"The airfield?" she queried.

He picked up the extension on the end table next to where he was standing.

"Hello?" His expression went flat. He held out the phone to her.

No-o-o. Micah had found her? Eden took it gingerly.

"Hello?"

"Why are you in a room registered to him?" Micah asked in his I'm-willing-to-be-reasonable-but-don't-waste-my-time voice.

"What have you been doing? Calling hotels?" Infuriating man!

"He caught me catching a rideshare to come here." Quinn's urgent voice sounded in the background.

"You're *here*?" Eden had texted Quinn after her shower, but that had been two snack baskets and two deeply disturbing conversations ago. "For God's sake, Micah. I am an adult."

"And as such, you will give me your room number and invite me up to speak with you," he said with false pleasantness. "Or meet us here in the lobby."

"Why are you so—" She stopped herself and clenched her teeth in frustration.

Part of her wanted to force the conversation he needed with Remy, but one glance at Remy and her heart juddered to a halt.

Remy was watching her closely. Outwardly, his expression was remote and unaffected, but she sensed the explosive tension gathering beneath his surface. He hadn't told her everything. She knew that instinctually.

She also knew that Micah would again accuse Remy of playing on her feelings and using her as an instrument against him. She wouldn't be able to hide from her brother that she had made love with Remy. She definitely couldn't stand here and listen to Micah berate him.

"Is the concierge there? Let me speak to them. I'll ask them to let you up."

A man's voice came on the line. She gave him their room number and hung up.

Still holding Remy's inscrutable look, she said, "We have to go."

CHAPTER SEVEN

EDEN RATTLED QUINN'S key fob onto the coffee table. Then—with a wild look of panic—retrieved the "honeymoon" basket from the bedroom.

Remy took it from her as she thrust it at him, even though he was not in the habit of fleeing with evidence from the scene of consensual lovemaking. Nor was he afraid of Micah. He had steeled himself to be around the man today, willing to keep their family history from overshadowing his best friend's wedding.

That was, of course, before he had taken Eden's virginity and courted an unplanned pregnancy. Somehow, he didn't think Eden's naive vision of his breaking bread and mending fences with her brother could be built on *that* new information. She was right. It was best he left.

He refused to leave her to make explanations on his behalf, though. He held the door while she hurriedly tied herself into her shoes.

The white heels didn't go with her outfit at all. They were embellished with sparkles and a satin ribbon that hung in a bow at her ankle, but they did what heels did and piled sex appeal onto an already knockout figure. Her hurried strides pulled at the narrow skirt so it slithered against her ass and thighs, and he saw a flash of her shins.

His fascination with her had gone far enough, however. The implications of what they'd done went beyond a possible pregnancy. He had only scratched the surface on the events of twenty-eight years ago when the rivalry between their families truly started, but some secrets were meant to stay buried.

He would worry about how to *keep* it buried if Eden actually turned up pregnant.

Eden set the internal locking lever so the door remained cracked as they left.

"I'll text Quinn to make herself at home." She turned away from the elevator. "We should take the stairs— Oh. That's convenient."

Midway along the hall, a wide, carpeted staircase led them down to a deserted, multi-function floor. It held a closed bar and a handful of locked breakout rooms. At the far end, there was an elevator that would take them straight to the parking level.

"I've been drinking," Remy recalled as she pushed the button for the basement. "My keys are with the valet." He set the basket on the floor of the elevator and pulled out his phone to call the front desk. There was a text from his pilot. "They're replacing the part right now. That answers where we're going."

"I'll tell Quinn I'm going to Toronto. Micah can meet me there if he's that anxious to see me." Eden sent her text and hurried from the elevator into the parking garage. "Hi! Hello! Excuse me!" Eden trotted forward a few steps, waving at a woman climbing into a hatchback. "Are you leaving? Would you be interested in driving us to the heliport for…" She glanced at her purse. "I think I have forty dollars. I don't carry much cash," she told Remy.

"Make it a hundred." He had a half dozen currencies on him at all times.

The woman warily agreed. Eden put her at ease on the short drive, encouraging her to share that she worked in catering and had two kids. Her husband worked at the US-Canada border. When she asked about their reason for needing a lift, Eden brushed away her question.

"It's a long story, but let me give you my

card. Please reach out if you need anything at all. I have a lot of resources at my disposal and you've been such a lifesaver."

"You realize she'll go to the press once she puts together who you are and what happened?" Remy asked as Eden waved her off. "Micah will know you left with me. Everyone will."

"The media storm is already throwing hailstones," she said starkly. "I authorized my assistant to confirm the wedding is off, but I have to prepare a press release so Hunter's people can coordinate with my team then...ugh. Ride it out, I suppose."

Him, too. Remy was realizing that it had been one thing to be seen with her in the moments after the wedding had fallen apart—that had been a favor to his friend—but any enterprising paparazzo could trace them to that hotel room and draw salacious conclusions.

"Oh, you're back," Andrea said as they strode into the heliport. "And you've changed." She waggled her eyebrows. "I guess you enjoyed the room."

Salacious like that. What the hell was wrong with some people? Eden blushed chokecherry-red and tried to stammer out a thank-you for the woman's earlier assistance.

Remy cut her off as he demanded, "Status of my machine?"

"I believe they're working on it," Andrea said, sobering as she read his dismay.

"Good." He grabbed Eden's hand and tugged her out to the tarmac with him, refusing to leave her there to suffer that woman's speculation even though his possessive, protective attitude basically confirmed they had "enjoyed" the room.

None of this was supposed to have happened. He was furious with himself and could only think that they needed to keep a lid on it. He couldn't drop her in Toronto to ride out the wait alone, though.

"The mechanic is finished, sir. We're fully fueled and can take off as soon as we're cleared by control," his pilot said.

"Good." Remy nodded for him to continue his preflight preparations and squeezed Eden's shoulder to draw her attention from the phone she was double-thumbing.

She lifted a distracted expression. Lines of tension had come in around her mouth and anxious shadows invaded her dark brown eyes.

"You were leaving for Greece directly from the wedding, weren't you? That means you have your passport?"

"I do." She hugged her purse under her arm. "Why?"

"Your home in Toronto will be staked out. I'll take you to Montreal. We'll fly from there."

Her eyes went wide with shock. "To where?"

"Martinique."

"I thought it was rainy season." She made it sound as though she'd caught him in a false-hood.

"That's why it's a quiet place to stay."

She blinked in befuddlement before her eye-brows came together with caution. "By my-self? Or…?"

"Together. But let's keep this—" He searched for a way to describe whatever this was between them. Obsession, maybe? Spend-ing more time with her certainly wouldn't help him dampen his lust, but that's what he would have to do. "I want to know as soon as you do. If nothing transpires—" he couldn't help the twist of his mouth as he found such a lovely euphemism for the hot mess they would be in if she was pregnant "—we go back to Plan A."

"One and done," she said in a hollow voice.

"Yes." He ignored the sharp knife of elec-tric heat that jolted through his chest and left a scorched sensation in the pit of his stomach.

"Sir?" His pilot closed the hatch, where he

had stowed Remy's bag, and opened the door to the passenger area of the helicopter.

Remy held out his hand.

Eden didn't know if she was being cowardly or desperate as she settled into the plush leather seat facing forward. Her phone was still blowing up with emails and voice messages that she was eager to avoid, but she felt bereft as Remy moved into the copilot's seat in the forward cabin.

He left the door open, but she was so sensitive, she felt rebuffed. The helicopter was close-quarters, not cramped. He could have taken the seat across from her without their knees touching beneath the table between them.

He didn't want to be with her, though.

If nothing transpires, we go back to Plan A.

She had agreed to that, but it seemed like a thousand hours ago. She had foolishly believed the ache of yearning for him would somehow be satisfied if she slept with him once. On the contrary, she now knew what he could make her feel and was even more drawn to him.

As the helicopter swayed ever so slightly as it lifted off, she looked toward the sliver of Remy that she could see—his shoulder and the headphone that covered his ear. She silently begged him to reveal again the man who had said, *I feel empty all the time.*

That's how she felt, so intensely hollow she could hardly breathe through the desolation.

That man had disappeared, though. He was distancing himself. Shutting down and shutting her out. He was trying to hide his association with her because he was embarrassed—ashamed?—to have slept with her.

This schism hurt so much, she ought to have insisted he take her home, where she could begin reassembling her life, but there was that other irrational part of her that would settle for this scant contact. For a few more days with him, remote as he might be.

Truthfully, he wasn't wrong to hide their relationship, such as it was. She wasn't ready to face whatever questions would come up if she went home. Her mother wouldn't understand this reckless desire that gripped her. Micah would see it as outright treason.

Which didn't make avoiding them right, but it certainly made it easier to put off the inevitable reckoning. Almost all of it. She had a press release to craft.

With a sigh, she picked up her phone again. Her PR team had suggested a slant that threw all the blame onto Hunter and the wedding crasher, Amelia.

Eden sidestepped taking such an easy way out. There was an innocent baby involved. She couldn't throw a single mom under the bus and, honestly, she didn't feel like a victim, just collateral damage.

As she glanced out the window, where the shadows of the rotors chopped across the sunlight, she considered how little rancor she felt toward Hunter. Today had been awful, but in some ways, she couldn't relate at all to the woman she had been this morning when she had been buttoned into her gown.

How had she imagined she could marry Hunter Waverly when Remy Sylvain existed in this world? Marrying anyone else seemed like a ridiculous delusion.

Not that she expected to marry Remy.

With a small sob, she slouched deeper into her seat.

Believing they were soul mates was a delusion, but as she lifted her gaze to the back of his shoulder again, she felt a nearly irresistible desire to move closer and touch him. Not to get his attention, simply to touch. To have the right to caress and share a moment of physical connection.

Why was she pulled so inexorably toward him?

And why was it so terrible for them to see if

they had more than sexual attraction? Remy's explanation about Micah's father had helped her understand a little, but it still seemed like an overreaction. She almost wished she had hung back to ask Micah why he continued to hold on to so much antipathy toward Remy? Because of her? She was fine.

Sort of.

She checked in with Quinn, texting to ask if Micah had blown his stack when they got to the empty hotel room. Three dots briefly came up, but disappeared just as quickly.

Eden thought about trying a video call, but she didn't know how to explain to her friend why she was fleeing the country with the one man no one would approve of. Better to focus on her press release.

She sent it to her assistant as they landed. Remy helped her down the steps to the tarmac and they walked directly across to a private jet painted in an abstract blend of metallic green, purple and tropical blue. Remy waved her to precede him up the stairs.

Inside, it looked more like an exclusive nightclub than an airplane. The furniture was low and cut along curved, ultramodern lines. The lighting was subdued gold, the colors mimicking white sand and blue-green seas. They moved past a dining nook with a wrap-around bench and Remy indicated one of the recliners that faced a big screen showing a welcome message and a Wi-Fi code.

He moved forward through an oval door that blinked like an eye, like something in a spaceship movie. Leaving her to travel alone again, she supposed.

She turned her pout to the window, where the midsummer sun was descending, turning the shadows long as the day stretched toward evening.

"Ms. Bellamy?" A male steward held a tray with a damp facecloth, a small dish of mint candies and a glass of ice water. "I'm Antoine. I'll be serving a meal once we're airborne, but may I bring you a refreshment before takeoff? Champagne? A cocktail, perhaps?"

"I would love a Caesar, but make it a mocktail, please." She kept the facecloth and the ice water, feeling modestly revived after she had washed her hands and rehydrated.

Remy returned as Antoine brought her drink.

"I'll have one of those," he said as he eyed her Caesar.

"Virgin?" Antoine asked.

"Promiscuous. As morally objectionable as you can make it."

Eden hid her smile against the spiced rim of

her drink, enjoying the tang of clam-flavored tomato juice with a shot of tabasco and a hint of dill.

Was that what she was now? No longer a virgin, therefore morally promiscuous? She turned a wistful glance to the window, unable to say she was sorry about it. The memory of their lovemaking brought goose bumps to her arms and shivers of pleasure all over her body.

She realized Remy's aloof gaze was fixed on her. She rubbed at her arms, cheeks stinging at how obvious she was.

"I should have got my suitcase from Quinn," she lied. "I hope there'll be some sort of shopping when we land?"

He opened a hatch beneath the television and shook out a sweater with wavy bands of sunset colors knitted into it.

"If that's too big, my sister may have left something in my stateroom."

The sweater was massive on her, but it smelled like him and felt so consoling, Eden snuggled herself into it. But—

"Is this *your* plane?" She realized he had changed into a lighter pair of pants and loafers without socks. "Like, not a charter or a corporate jet?"

"Why is that surprising?" He took his seat, stowing his phone into the cup holder without looking, as if it was something he'd done thousands of times. "I own a fleet."

"I guess that's why I'm surprised. I assumed you would jump aboard a flight whenever you need to, not keep one parked like a car in the garage."

"My sister occasionally steals the keys," he said dryly. "The rest of the family fly standby, but my schedule requires more flexibility so I keep this ready."

Antoine brought Remy's drink. "If you're comfortable, sir, the pilot has instructed me to buckle in for takeoff?"

Remy nodded and Antoine disappeared through the spaceship door.

"You sound like you're close with your sister," Eden mused gently, wanting to know more about him. As the president of Can-Carib Airlines, Remy had a presence online that was heavily curated toward business reporting, but was readily available to access. The rest of his family seemed elusive by comparison.

"We are." He took another long sip and exhaled to cool whatever burn it had lit in his throat. "She texted me earlier, asking if I would take her to France with me. My aunt and uncle are celebrating their fortieth wedding anniversary next week. I told her I was headed to Martinique and would leave from there. She's in

New York so she'll have to find her own way." He tapped his glass with one pensive finger.

"You'll, um, go without me? If we don't know by then?" Eden was a big girl. There was no reason she should feel so abandoned.

"We'll see, won't we?" He flashed her a look. "I imagine you'll dominate the gossip sites for the next week or two."

"For what it's worth, I didn't mention you in my press release. Have you texted Hunter? Does he know we're—" Her heart swerved away from the word *together*. "That you're helping me?"

His mouth flattened. "That can wait."

It's not like he'll care, she wanted to say. She looked out the window to hide the dampness that rose against her lashes. She'd been so frustrated by this long day, she could hardly keep tears from overflowing.

When she had control of herself, she texted her team that she was taking her honeymoon time as vacation and instructed them to schedule a board meeting for her return. Then she checked in with her mother and her brother, telling them the same thing.

Her mother texted back, Micah said you left with Remy Sylvain. Are you home?

Eden glanced across at him. No. He helped

me avoid paparazzi by flying me to Montreal.
Now we're—

She backspaced.

Now I'm on a plane to the Caribbean.

Where, exactly? I'll meet you.

Eden chewed her lip, reluctant to tell her
mother that she was with Remy. Lucille would
disapprove. She was sure of it. When Eden
had returned from Paris five years ago, deeply
hurt by the belief that Remy had targeted her,
her mother had grilled her in a way that had
seemed like maternal concern at the time, but
now Eden wondered.

"Put it behind you," Lucille had insisted before she had a long conversation with Micah
behind a closed door.

Lucille had also been concerned when Eden
had revealed that Remy was Hunter's best man.
"What did he say?"

"He acted like we'd never met."

"Then you should do the same," Lucille had
said firmly. "Let sleeping dogs lie."

Eden wished she could ask her mother for
more details on what might have transpired between Remy and Micah's fathers, but Lucille
rarely talked about her first husband. Eden

doubted her mother would tell her anything, so it wasn't worth stirring up old hurts.

I need some time alone, Eden texted. To work out how to solve the BH&G situation.

It was an open-ended nudge for her mother to relent and allow Micah to help, but her mother only replied, I'm sure you'll come up with something. Let me know when you've landed safely.

Eden put her phone away, thinking her mother had more faith in her resourcefulness than she did in herself.

CHAPTER EIGHT

A CRACK OF thunder and a flash of lightning had Eden sitting up with a gasp.

For a moment, she was dizzy and disoriented, heart racing with alarm. Slowly she made sense of the furniture illuminated by the dim glow from the night-light she'd left on in the adjoining bathroom.

Martinique. Remy.

She closed her eyes in a twinge of disgrace, both in going away with him and for putting herself in a position of needing to. The debacle of her wedding flew straight onto the pile of her chagrin, along with the weight of BH&G.

Her entire life was a scorched, sticky mess and she was alone in the middle of it.

Without checking, she knew the other side of the mattress was empty, not that she had expected Remy to have come to bed with her. Did she want him to? She shouldn't, but she felt tremendously lonely.

At least during the flight, Remy's steady presence had kept the worst of the doom at bay. They had eaten spinach-and-artichoke puff pastries in their seats along with rice cups that held a scrumptious bite of tandoori chicken. Then they moved to the dining table for their main course, roasted lobster with whipped parsnips and a watercress salad. They finished with a light strawberry mousse.

After that, they watched a forgettable action movie, then, just as she was nodding off, they began their descent. The rain had eased and the freshly washed night had reflected the sparkling lights of Fort-de-France.

"There's something magical about arriving somewhere at night, isn't there?" she had said dreamily as the hatch was opened and a fresh breeze wafted across her face. "It's like a Christmas present still in its wrapper. You can't tell what's inside and you have to wait to find out."

"That's very poetic. Are you secretly a romantic?"

Since that hadn't been the first time she'd been accused of being one, it probably wasn't a secret, but she deflected, and said, "I've never been to the Caribbean before. It feels exciting."

"We have a few nightclubs, but on the whole, island culture tends to be very laid-back." He walked her to a wine-red convertible waiting on the tarmac for them.

"Different, then," she said once they were nestled inside it. "I've been to Florida for the amusement parks, and Micah brought me to Europe two or three times a year. I've seen Mediterranean beaches, but most of my family vacations were in Canada. BH and G's motto is 'It's great to be home…and garden' so camping in the Rockies was more on-brand than visiting a tropical all-inclusive. I'm dying for sun and sand."

"Sand, I can promise, including in places you don't want it," he said dryly as he steered the car onto a highway. "Sunshine will be hit-and-miss."

Traffic had been light and Remy knew the roads. He had zipped in and around other cars, taking a route inland that climbed and wound into dense tropical forest before descending toward an expanse of black ocean and charcoal clouds on the horizon.

Her arduous day must have caught up with her because the next thing she knew, Remy had asked, "Are you awake?"

The car had been parked and her cheek had tingled with the sensation of a light caress.

"Do you want me to carry you in?"

Of course, she did. She wanted to be coddled and petted and told everything would be all right.

"Don't be silly." She'd walked into the villa, taking in an impression of burnt-orange shutters against Tuscan-yellow walls and a wrap-around veranda.

Had she also heard the rush of waves? If so, it was muffled now by the rumble of thunder and the steady patter of rain on the roof.

She was thirsty, so she rose and retied the sarong she'd worn to bed.

This was Remy's sister's room. He had told her to help herself to whatever she needed, but his sister was a fashion designer and most of the clothes looked to be her own creations. They seemed too well-tailored and personal to borrow. Eden had limited herself to the sarong and a silk sleep bonnet still in its package.

She padded out and followed the soft glow toward the living room.

The villa wasn't as extravagant as she had expected, given the luxury of the jet. It was more of a charming bungalow, reminding her of her Grammy Bellamy's farmhouse in its eclectic, comfortable decor. Eden nudged a rattan rocking chair on her way through the living room and picked up a mango from the bowl on the dining-room table to smell it.

Oh! Family photos.

She moved behind the table to study the mosaic of framed photographs on the wall.

There was Remy, maybe five years old, deeply tanned and wearing a checkered shirt and a big smile as he held an infant she presumed was his sister. His parents were a cute pair of young professionals in double-breasted suits with thick shoulder pads, looking fondly on their children. Other relatives were captured in dated photos wearing fashions from bygone decades. In one beautifully framed, hand-colored photograph, a couple stood in formal attire from the early 1900s, their expressions somber.

"Do you need something?"

"Oh." Her heart flipped as she turned. She self-consciously touched the sleep bonnet.

Damn. Remy was wearing hardly anything at all, just drawstring shorts tied low on his hips and a whole lot of naked skin over well-toned muscles. Her gaze swept down to the narrow trail of hair below his navel and jerked back upward.

She swallowed and crossed her arms to secure the sarong, instantly aware of her nakedness beneath the light cotton.

"A glass of water?" She lifted a sheepish shoulder since there was an L-shaped counter between her and the sink. "I couldn't resist looking at the photos. This is a family home?"

"My father's grandparents built the original and raised their children here." He moved to the kitchen, where he'd left a light burning over the stove. He opened a cupboard to the left of it. "We modernized ten years ago, but the laws are strict when it comes to exterior changes. We were more interested in preserving what we love than turning it into a palace, anyway. My sister and I are the only ones who use it. Tap okay? Or would you prefer bottled?"

"Tap is fine." She followed him into the kitchen and accepted the glass he poured. "Do you spend a lot of time here?"

"As much as I can, given the size of Can-Carib and my many responsibilities and other family obligations. My father's relatives are here so I try to visit a few times a year. I share a housekeeper with my aunt. She'll know I'm here and will expect me to drop by."

That sounded like a warning. Eden lowered her glass.

"Will the housekeeper tell her you're not alone?"

He leaned his hips on the counter and folded his arms across his bare chest, drawing her eye to the curve of his biceps and the ball of his shoulder. The compulsion to set her lips against his burnished skin was nearly irresistible.

"She might. And since I've never brought a woman here before, I imagine she'll read into it."

Eden tried to swallow past a sudden dryness in her throat. *Don't think that makes you special*, she cautioned herself. He had only brought her here for expediency's sake.

"What will you say if she finds out?"

"I don't know." His mouth twisted.

Another crack of lightning made her jump. Thunder rattled like a convoy of semitrailers across the roof.

She looked up with alarm while the lights flickered.

"You should be here during a hurricane."

"Have you?"

"Yes. And I take back recommending it. It's exciting in the wrong way."

She liked that quirk of his mouth when he was being ironic. Their gazes caught and locked. Whether it was the gathering of ions outside, working toward another lightning strike, or the ever-present chemistry between them, she didn't know, but the air became charged. All of her pricked and her lungs grew tight.

"Is it not fair to say that you're helping me

dodge a publicity problem?" she asked, feeling the tension that flexed in her throat. "That that's all this is?"

"Sure," he drawled. "I can give that a try."

"Your aunt won't buy it? Because it's not as if we're...carrying on." Had she really used one of Grammy's old-fashioned expressions?

If she was honest, she definitely wanted to carry on. Longing was buffeting her like those winds outside, gusting and pushing and swirling—

The world went black. Utterly absent of light.

Above them, the cascade of rain on the roof increased.

She blinked and widened her eyes, but saw absolutely nothing.

"I left my cellphone in the bedroom." She reached for the edge of the counter, planning to set down her water. Her fingers bumped into the warm skin of Remy's tense abdomen.

He caught her hand, held it firmly.

"Mine is in my room, too." His voice was tight.

He started past her, but she held on to his hand, shuffling behind him past the furniture and into the hall. She trailed her free hand along the wall as they made their way past the opening to the first room. It had looked like an office when she had briefly glanced in on her way to the kitchen.

He stopped and held her from bumping into him with a light pressure on the hand he still held. "Can you get to the bed from here?"

She could feel the heat radiating off him. Her ears were trying to pick apart his tone. Was he angry?

"I wonder if this is what it feels like to be untethered in deep space," she mused, hand reaching into the nothingness.

"We have oxygen."

Yet she couldn't breathe. As metaphors went, the vacuum of space epitomized her future. Formless and empty. Unsurvivable.

"I'll get my phone so you can see," he said.

Before he could step away, without letting herself overthink it, she turned into the only thing that felt real. Him. She reached for his strength and pressed herself into his warmth, sliding her arms around his waist. Her face found the hard plane of his chest and she rubbed her cheek against the taut silk of his skin.

"Eden." Her name was a tight, hot roar of fire.

"I'm sorry." Her chin grazed his hard nipple as she tried to push away.

He didn't let her go. His arms clamped around her. "I can't take another chance."

"I know. I just wanted to feel you."

"Feel, then," he said in a guttural voice. He scraped her hands across his chest and swept them behind his back again. Then he cupped her face with his firm palm and his mouth was on hers. Hungry. So hungry she moaned in ecstasy at feeling her own yearning echoed back to her in this greedy, encompassing kiss.

It felt stolen, kissing like this in the pitch-dark. His image formed in her mind from her questing hands. From the indent of his spine and the firm globes of his butt and the ripples of his rib cage as she trailed her hands across him. She found the taut tendon connecting his neck and shoulder. His earlobes were as neatly formed as the rest of him. His tight curls prick-led her palm as she pressed the back of his head, urging a deeper kiss.

He seemed equally determined to discover and memorize, squeezing and caressing as he swept his hands across her back, hips, breasts and waist.

"Let's find the bed," she urged.

Instead, he slipped away from her. His lips touched her collarbone, then he was sliding from the arms she had twined around his neck.

She sobbed with loss, only to realize he was

dropping to his knees. Her back met the door-jamb. Her sarong was an ephemeral thing that was brushed away like a bridal veil. His mouth branded kisses across her abdomen and across the tops of her thighs and into the aching center of her.

Gasping with acute pleasure, she clung to his shoulders and moved with the rhythm of his kiss, moaning unashamedly, thrilling and rising so quickly to her peak, it ought to have been embarrassing, but it was too good. Too, too good.

He didn't stop. She was still pulsing in climax as he pressed his finger inside her. He continued kissing and laving, and the gentle thrusting of his finger drove her to an even higher pinnacle. She nearly screamed when she arrived.

Shaking, she would have collapsed, but he rose to gather her and somehow shuffled to the bed and set her on the rumpled covers.

With a half laugh of bemused joy, she stroked her touch over his arms, eager to feel his weight come down upon her. She wanted him *in* her.

He evaporated into the dark.

"Sleep. I'll see you in the morning." His words rasped across her sensitized nerves.

"Remy." She sucked in a breath of betrayal

and rose onto her elbow, but only heard the door closing behind him.

Pressing her still trembling thighs together, she rolled onto her side, hugged a pillow and buried her crumpling face into it.

After feverishly appeasing the lust-driven barbarian within him—alone, with his fist—Remy slept in. He woke with a head full of sawdust and recriminations ripe in the back of his throat.

In those sightless, humid moments in the night, he had told himself it was enough that he didn't risk another pregnancy, but his attempt to slake his thirst for her had only been stimulated, not satisfied. He wanted her more than ever.

He stepped under a blast of cold water, swore, but was no longer erect, so he dressed and followed the aroma of coffee to the kitchen.

Beyond the open doors to the veranda, the sun shone brightly on the thick tropical vegetation that spilled bright blooms around the gazebo. The rest of the backyard was mostly sand and almond trees, with a boardwalk beneath their shady branches that led to the beach.

Eden stood in the open wooden gate at the end, facing the ocean. She had switched out last night's bonnet for a yellow-and-blue head wrap and had changed into one of his sister's T-shirts and a pair of loose board shorts, both a size too big.

Remy heard a noise and realized it was him, groaning. He only needed to look at Eden and he was right back to wanting to touch and taste and take. Last night had been the backslide of an addict, but oh, had it been worth it. Her trembling thighs and writhing hips and cries of exaltation had nearly tipped him over the edge, all from touching her, not himself.

Somehow, he'd kept himself from taking yet another reckless chance, but craving her had returned with a vengeance.

So stupid. It wasn't fair to say she had reached for him first, either. He knew she was going through a lot. He never should have let it get as far as it had. It was a damn miracle he had walked away last night, but he had heard her gasp of shock right before he'd closed the door between them. She had been hurt by his exit.

He had turned what could have been a tense, but civilized, sharing of a living space into a powder keg of bottled emotions.

There was no hiding from it, though. He poured himself a coffee and walked down to join her.

"Thinking of starting your day with a swim?" he asked as he came up behind her.

She stiffened and sipped the coffee she held, eyes staying on the ocean.

"Maybe later, when it's hotter. I don't feel like being cold and wet right now." Her voice was thin and strained.

His ears rang, hearing too much significance in that statement. Then he thought, screw it. He wasn't going to pick apart what they'd done or leave himself open to jabs.

"Your Canadian is showing," he said and set his cup on the top of the gatepost. He brushed past her, striding unhesitatingly down the kelp-littered beach and into the surf.

The water here was always a tepid, silky bath. Diving into a wave submerged him in homecoming, washing away whatever troubles had driven him to the place of his roots.

Today, his troubles waded cautiously into the water behind him.

"It's warm!" she said with an astonished smile that hit his heart like an exploding rainbow.

"You said you'd been to the Med. It's warm, isn't it?"

"Sure, but I've also been in the Atlantic. I never got past here in PEI." She cut the side of her palm against the outside of her thigh. "This is fabulous."

She sank to her shoulders. Her head bobbed as a wave rolled in to pick her up and move her toward the beach.

They swam for twenty minutes before they waded ashore. The T-shirt hung off her shoulders and clung to her chest. She plucked it away so her bra wasn't so visible through the fabric, but he'd seen it. It was imprinted in his brain now, exactly the way she was. Indelibly.

"Iguana," he said, forcing his gaze down the beach and pointing.

"Get out." She walked a little closer to the driftwood, where the stocky, brownish-gray lizard was perched. Waves rhythmically frothed around their shins. "Do they bite?"

"I've never been close enough to find out. He'll disappear pretty— There he goes." It skittered up the beach into the brush, leaving only slither marks in the sand.

"Too bad they didn't see it." She looked toward some children who were coming onto the beach with their father. Tourists, Remy surmised, since he didn't recognize them. "This was your childhood? Swimming before breakfast and spotting lizards?"

"This was my winter. I don't even know what a white Christmas is."

"Lucky."

He was. He knew that. But not always, he thought, as her profile grew troubled again.

"Can I ask you something?" It had been bothering him since the hotel room.

"What?" She lifted her gaze and wary shadows came into her expression.

"Why did you want to marry Hunter if you didn't love him?"

"Oh." She looked at her feet, bending to pick up a broken shell. "Lots of reasons, all very practical. Being impetuous has never served me well. Where's the harm in meeting a man at a nightclub?" She lifted a disparaging eyebrow. "Where's the harm in sleeping with him *once*?"

Once. His heart swerved. He didn't look at her, but he knew she wasn't looking at him, either. That word—*once*—had been closing like walls around him, suffocating him in its limitations. That's what last night had been. Once *more*.

So foolish, but he couldn't seem to regret it. Not enough to swear it wouldn't happen again.

"Being impetuous got my mother into trouble. Literally. The same kind," she added with amused despair. "A tale as old as time, right?"

"Is that why she married Gould? She was pregnant with Micah?"

"Yes. She was a small-town prairie girl backpacking in Europe with a friend. He swept her off her feet and she immediately turned up pregnant. She was so relieved when he agreed to marry her, but she quickly regretted it."

"Abusive?" he asked with a stab of suspicion. Stronger than suspicion. Fatalistic certainty.

"I'm not sure about physically." She frowned into the distance. "She doesn't talk about him. My take is that he was very insidious in how he dismantled her self-worth. His family piled on. Mama wasn't born into money and private education and aristocratic lineage. His parents thought she was a gold digger. They insisted she have a nanny, then Kelvin used that against her when she left him, saying she had never bonded with Micah in the first place."

Kelvin Gould had been a monster.

"When did she leave?" Remy was pretty sure he knew, but he wondered if Eden did.

"When he cheated. Of course, the prenup favored him." She worked her thumb on the smooth inside of the shell she still held. "She signed it very naively, believing him when he said it would protect her. She wasn't entitled to anything and didn't want his money, anyway. She wanted to bring Micah to Canada. She didn't have any money of her own, though.

Nothing for a lawyer and no qualifications to get a job that paid well enough to afford one. She had to work minimum-wage, entry-level stuff. Kelvin said she couldn't support Micah in the standard he was entitled to and left him in Austria with his own parents. He threatened such an ugly fight, Mama settled for Micah visiting a few times a year, when Kelvin deigned to send Micah to her. Her boss found her crying about it one day. He bought her a coffee and a few days later he gave her a promotion and a raise."

"Your father?" Remy asked, guessing.

"Yes." Eden smiled with affection. "They still didn't know each other that well when he proposed. Mama wasn't keen at first, having already been in a marriage that went south, but Dad could see how desperate she was to have Micah in her life. He loved her practically at first sight—"

Her voice faltered briefly and Remy's breath stopped in his lungs, but maybe she'd just been affected by discussing the loss of her father. He didn't even believe in things like love at first sight, let alone imagine it was hereditary.

"Dad was also very pragmatic and sensible, so it wasn't the same whirlwind that had got Mama into such a bad situation with Kelvin. Dad wanted a family and they already worked

well together. He said if she married someone as well respected and wealthy as he was,
she would have more leverage against Kelvin,
which was true. She was able to fly him over
more often and eventually got him to live with
us. Briefly."

Her voice halted again as she perhaps remembered what he'd told her about that time.

"Anyway, they loved each other very deeply.
That encouraged me to believe I could have the
same strong and healthy marriage if I found
the right sort of partner."

Was that really what she wanted? Something about that didn't ring true. He couldn't
claim to know her well, but she was lively and
whimsical and had leaped into his car very
impetuously. She was here with him, barely
twenty-four hours after she was supposed to
marry another man, and could possibly be
pregnant with his child.

Eden struck him as someone who led with
her heart. It didn't make sense that she would
settle for a dispassionate and pragmatic arrangement. No, Remy was sure she would prefer to marry for love.

"Bonjour," she called warmly in French.

They had come up to the children, who were
turning over a rock.

"What have you found? A sea star? Oh, a

baby crab." Eden expressed the right amount of fascination. They invited her up the beach to see some other small wonders.

Their father hung back with Remy, asking if it was safe to let the children swim or if there were rip currents to watch for.

Remy said it was safe and gave him tips on where to snorkel and hike with his young family.

He was absently keeping one eye on Eden and the children as they bent to examine a pool of water. Eden was smiling as she rose to stand, but her expression dropped into a surprised sort of blankness. She staggered once and her knees collapsed.

"Eden!" Remy started running, but couldn't get any traction in the sand.

Even as she put out a hand to catch herself, she crumpled limply to the beach.

"Eden!"

The children stood wide-eyed as Remy dropped to his knees beside her. He rolled her onto her back. She was completely unconscious. Breathing, at least, but his own lungs had shrunk to airless sacks. His entire body flooded with adrenaline.

"What happened? Did something sting her?" The father came up, breathless.

The children shook their heads, fearful.

"Run to that house with the red gate." Remy pointed. "Tell Celeste that Remy needs her." Would she be home? It was Sunday. Church.

Damn it.

He touched the backs of his fingers to Eden's cheek. Heat exhaustion? There was still a fresh morning breeze, not the full humid heat of the afternoon.

He examined her hands and feet, looking for bites or scratches. His mind was running through all that they'd eaten. She hadn't had breakfast yet. Was it low blood sugar? Was she diabetic?

Why didn't he know everything about her?

"Come on, Eden." He squeezed her shoulder. *"Wake up."*

CHAPTER NINE

"REMY!"

Eden heard someone call his name, but was too confused to make sense of who it could be. She was on a warm, lumpy bed that was both comfortable and not. Cool, but in a nice way.

She opened her eyes and sunlight shot straight into the back of her brain, causing spots behind her eyelids, which she'd reflexively clenched against the brightness.

How many people had she seen? Three? Four? Remy and some children?

"No," she groaned, recalling how her vision had gone white. "Did I faint?"

"*Yes.* No. Stay there." Remy's heavy hand pressed her shoulder, forcing her to remain on the sand. "This is my auntie Celeste. She's a doctor. This is Eden, Auntie."

Eden peeked against the sun and glimpsed a buxom woman in her late sixties wearing a yellow dress and a madras headscarf. She was sinking down to one knee beside Eden.

"Bonjour, Eden. Let me check your pulse."

"I'm okay," Eden insisted. "Please don't be alarmed."

"I'm actually retired." Celeste picked up her wrist. "Too old to be running down a beach, so let's both take a moment to catch our breath." She took a slow inhale, rolling her free hand to encourage Eden to breathe with her.

They took three or four breaths together, then Celeste released Eden's wrist.

"Your pulse is a little weak."

"I'm fine. Honestly," Eden insisted.

"Pregnant?"

"No."

"Possibly," Remy corrected grimly.

Celeste's glance toward Remy conveyed about a thousand questions, emotions and layers of parental disapproval, but her voice remained reassuring as she asked, "How far along would you be, Eden?"

"It's low blood pressure," Eden said with a grimace of embarrassment. "It's not serious. It happens sometimes when it's hot, if I stand up too fast. I take salt pills, but…" She risked a glance at Remy. "I didn't take them for the last week because I didn't want to retain any water." For the wedding.

Remy made a noise of disgust and pushed to his feet, looking as though he was warming up to lecture her into a watery grave.

"You need an electrolyte replacer," Celeste said.

"I have some tablets at the house." Remy helped both her and Celeste to stand. "Thanks for coming, Auntie. We won't keep you." He kissed her cheek.

"You'll come for dinner. I'll cook for you after church." Her stern look at Remy suggested he could use some churching himself.

"We'll be there," he promised, but Eden could feel the tension radiating off him. She wasn't sure if it was because he was still rattled by her fainting, or by what he'd let slip to his aunt.

"See, I'm fine," Eden reassured the children with a smile. "Maybe I'll see you here tomorrow."

If she survived whatever fallout was about to happen from Remy's blurted announcement.

"Will she tell anyone?" Eden asked him when they were back in his home and Remy was stirring rehydration tablets into a glass of water.

"She doesn't gossip, especially about someone's health history, but she'll have questions." He handed her the fizzing glass and began efficiently preparing breakfast, setting fish cakes the housekeeper had left into a frying pan and chopping mango that he put in bowls with yogurt and muesli.

She should have offered to help, but the last thing she needed was to bump elbows with him again. She sat at the dining table, where she could watch him without being too obvious about it.

"What will you tell her?" she asked.

"It's more what she'll tell me," he said sardonically. "She's my father's older sister, the matriarch on his side of the family and traditional in her views. That's a Catholic church she's attending today. She sees it as her place to ensure I live my life right and she also misses my father. She wants to see him reflected in the next generation. That means I ought to marry and start producing little Sylvains. I respect all of that."

But not with you, Eden heard silently tacked onto the end of that.

I can't take another chance, he had said last night. He hadn't wanted to up their risk of pregnancy.

For a few minutes on the beach, she had quit obsessing over what had happened between them and simply enjoyed what the morning and his world had to offer. Now her thoughts were drifting back to what had almost felt like a dream, if she hadn't awakened to see her half-empty glass of water on the counter.

"Can I take your car after breakfast? I need to pick up a few things," she said, purely because she needed an escape from this pressured awareness.

"Salt tablets?" he asked.

"And clothes. Maybe a laptop so I can work. A salon." She could take out the clip-in extensions herself. She had planned to do it on the flight to Greece, but what she really needed was space and time away from him.

"My sister has one she likes. I'll make a call to get you in. I'll take you to the boutiques she likes, too. Let me know the specs on the laptop. I'll see what I can find while you're getting your hair done."

Great. More time together.

"Finish that," he said sternly, as she started to set aside her glass.

"It's honestly not a big deal. I've fainted on a beach before and I still live a rich and fulfilling life." She had also fainted in the shower once and wound up with a goose egg, but she kept that to herself.

She broke their staring contest first, noticing in the daylight that the wall of photos had an empty hook. Weird.

The buzz of Remy's phone and the cynical snort he released distracted her from asking about it, though.

"What's wrong?" she asked.

"Hunter is asking if I still want to be his best man."

"He's marrying that woman?" Amelia? Was that her name?

"Tomorrow."

"Wow." It wasn't that shocking, but it was awfully fast. And it really blew out the last candle on the Hunter-will-save-BH&G cake.

"Are you upset?"

"No." She caught him eyeing her with skepticism and realized with a crumple of her last shred of pride that she would have to tell him the rest. "I had another reason for marrying him. BH and G is in trouble. Serious trouble. He knew," she said quickly as Remy's eyebrows shot up. "We talked about it when we started dating. He and I worked out that expansion of his network technology using our store properties as part of our marriage agreement."

"RuralReach. That's off now?"

"My team is confident they can rescue it, but new terms will have to be worked out. It's definitely delayed. Hunter was planning a substantial investment as well. I was okay with sharing ownership with him when I was planning to have his children. Now he's just another business partner and I'm less comfortable allowing him so much influence in my company." She swirled the dregs of the hydration tablet in the last of her water and knocked it back. "That will happen, anyway, if I can't come up with another option, though."

"Why hasn't your brother bailed you out?"

"Mama refuses to let him! She has scruples against taking Kelvin's money even though he's *dead*." She rubbed at a chip in her nail polish. "I won't go against her wishes, though. I'm having some of our personal properties assessed, but that takes time and probably won't raise enough capital. Not as fast as we need it, anyway."

"Are you asking for my help?" He brought their dishes to the table.

"*No.* I'm arming you with a reason to tell your aunt why we can't marry. I'm a money pit."

"What if you're pregnant?"

"I didn't plan for that condom to break, Remy."

"I know that," he said evenly, reaching back for the cutlery before taking his seat. "I'm simply exploring what might happen if you are."

"Marrying for money did not work out for me," she noted bitterly.

"Because you didn't marry."

"Quit acting like this is something you would consider doing!"

"I'm obliged by my position as president of Can-Carib Airlines to evaluate all opportunities that are presented to me. Hunter is a shrewd businessman. He wouldn't tie himself to a sinking ship. There must have been benefits that went beyond using the Bellamy name to clean up Wave-Com's reputation." His flickering gaze across her shoulders and throat said, *Besides the obvious.*

Her stomach pitched.

"Will you send me the contract so I can review it?" he asked.

"What are you thinking? Travel agencies within the store to book tropical vacations? I don't see it, especially out west. Hawaii is a shorter flight and Mexico is cheaper. Also, our brand is stay-cation. Camping and outdoor sports like hiking and hockey."

"Martinique's economy is too reliant on tourism. It needs to diversify. A fresh distribution market through a trusted franchise in Canada would allow the export sector to expand."

"Hmm." She tucked her chin in her hand. "My father always played the buy-Canadian card. It was the way we differentiated ourselves from the big-box, lowest-price chains. Things are so global now, it's been hard to stick to that. What kind of products would we carry?"

"Let's see." He looked to the ceiling. "Spices. Hammocks. Plants," he said with a tone of discovery. "'Can't get away this winter? Bring a taste of the tropics into your home with an orchid or a hibiscus.'"

"'Bring the garden into your home.' That works." She nodded. "But are you really willing to throw a pile of your own money at my company to make that happen? A *lot* of money?"

His expression shuttered and he stabbed a bite of fish cake. "If you're pregnant with my child? Absolutely."

If she was pregnant. Her heart twisted and she looked to her own meal.

Back to wait and see.

Remy could have left Eden at the pharmacy, but he stuck around to ensure they had what she needed to increase her blood pressure. Once he was reassured she wouldn't faint again, he left. The salon was only a block away and he had to drive across the island to the computer store.

He brooded the entire way.

He was glad to finally understand why Eden and Hunter had gotten as far as they had, but he was also annoyed. He was really freaking irritated that Hunter had roped her into an arranged marriage to save her business, then left her in the lurch. He was even more irritated that he cared. It was not his job to solve her romantic or business problems.

On the other hand, if he did have a baby with her, he wanted to be prepared. While he waited for the laptop, he sent some messages, setting up a discreet team to explore opportunities with Bellamy Home and Garden and forwarding to them the copy of the marriage contract she had sent him.

Marriage. He already knew that's what Auntie Celeste would suggest. It was very much her belief that if you took a chance on making a life with someone, you ought to be prepared to make a life with them.

In other circumstances, he would be.

Remy shook off that childish wish. *This* was his circumstance. It wasn't only his aversion to her brother, or the promises he had made to his father and himself, promises to love and protect and support his family. He wasn't a perfectionist—okay, he was—but he forgave himself the mistake of kissing Eden years ago. He hadn't known who she was then.

He expected more honorable behavior from himself now, though. Still, he had made love to her, knowing she was off-limits, and he was her *first* lover. That came with its own set of expectations he hadn't been prepared to meet.

Last night? What the hell was that if not pure self-indulgence? He could rationalize all he wanted that they hadn't risked pregnancy again, but what he had done was not exactly heroic.

Eden was dangerous to him. She had hung around in his head for years and, when he was around her, he abandoned his core principles. If she wasn't pregnant, he definitely couldn't marry her.

If she was... Hell, he didn't know what he would do.

He was still ruminating on her and self-control and what made a man a man as he visited the bakery near her salon, then set his purchases in the back seat of his open convertible.

His masculine eye was snagged by a woman walking toward him, swinging a few shopping bags. The wide skirt of her simple blue dress stopped midcalf and a line of buttons all the way down the front broke up the block of color. Her lips were painted a shimmery pink,

178 WEDDING NIGHT WITH THE WRONG BILLIONAIRE

her eyes were behind cat's-eye sunglasses and her hair was in shoulder-length braids.

His whole body twisted with such craving, he had to bite back a groan. Maybe he hadn't recognized Eden right away, but his body had. Her. It always had to be her.

"Perfect timing." Eden set her bags in the trunk as he popped it. "That's everything, except I'd like to get something for your aunt."

"Done." He pointed toward the back seat.

"Merci." She shook back her braids. The gold cuffs on the ends clicked together cheerfully. "I love that everyone speaks French here. Well, and Creole, obviously. I overheard some at the salon, but didn't catch any of it. I'd love to learn, though. I think I love everything about this place."

She radiated such happiness, he wanted to taste it. He wanted to cup her face and seal his mouth to hers and drink up her bubbly bliss. He wanted to kiss the hell out of her in the middle of the street.

He moved to open her door. "We should get home and unpackage your laptop. They always have to run a bunch of updates before they're any use."

Her bright mood faded slightly, but she only nodded as she slipped into her seat. "Good advice."

Yeah, he was chock-full of practical ideas. Too bad he wasn't capable of following any.

"Can I help with anything?" Eden offered when they arrived to find Celeste cooking on her outdoor stove.

"No, you sit. I make this fricassee in my sleep." Celeste waved her to the patio, where there was a table with four regular chairs and a rocker nearby. She had changed into a more casual, loose-fitting dress and had switched to a lightweight turban-style head wrap in robin's-egg blue.

"You're supposed to ask the housekeeper to cook," Remy reminded her, dropping a peck on her cheek. He reared back right before he got a wooden spoon in the kisser.

"Flore-Aline cooks for company. I cook for family. Fetch the salad from the refrigerator. Wait." She eyed the boxes he was carrying. "What did you bring me?"

"Macarons."

"That's why you're my favorite nephew. Take them inside or I'll eat them now. Tell me about yourself, Eden." She turned her wide smile on her.

Eden leaped at the opportunity to reassure Celeste that she and Remy were *just friends*. She gave her an abbreviated version of her

wedding disaster, playing up the drama of
Amelia arriving with a baby, and turned it into
a joke at her own expense.

"As you can imagine, my groom disappeared very *unceremoniously*."

Celeste chuckled, appreciating the pun, but
shook her head, agog. "That was *yesterday*?"

"Yes." It seemed like a lifetime ago.

Remy appeared with a round of water and
gave Eden one with the orange fizz of yet another electrolyte tablet. Seriously, Celeste was
going to ask her next if she had a UTI because
he had become Mr. Hydration and it was going
right through her.

Eden obediently sipped and made sure he
saw it before she continued.

"Remy was kind enough to save me from
the worst of the publicity by bringing me here."

"Oh? Are you famous?" Celeste paused in
her cooking to look at her.

"Not really. My father's father had a number
of radio shows throughout his life, so the Bellamy name is familiar in broadcasting circles.
Years ago, he recruited my mother to a call-in
show for gardening tips. She still does it, but
it's more a promo thing for the family's chain
of home-and-garden stores. I recently inherited
the company. No, the *famous* one—maybe I
should call him infamous?—was my groom.

Actually, do you know Hunter Waverly?" Eden cocked her head. "Remy's friend?"

"You were marrying Hunter Waverly?" Celeste's voice went up several octaves and she shot a look at Remy. "Would he be the father of your—" Her spoon drew a circle in the general vicinity of Eden's middle.

"No," Eden and Remy said together.

"It's complicated, Auntie," Remy added.

"I'll bet."

Eden bit her lips together and kept her gaze on the paving stones beneath Celeste's feet.

Celeste went back to her pans and soon dished up. Conversation switched to lighter topics while they enjoyed a delicious meal of conch fricassee with rice and spicy avocado balls.

Afterward, Eden excused herself to the washroom. She heard Remy's and Celeste's murmured voices through the open window, but they were speaking Creole. She wished she knew what he was saying, but supposed it was best to let him make their explanations however he saw fit.

She came out of the washroom and was confronted by a fresh wall of family photos. She immediately became lost. Why these sorts of displays fascinated her so much, she wasn't sure, but she was always a sucker for them.

Maybe it was because both her grandmothers had had them. They felt like home.

They also told interesting stories with their fashions and hairstyles, the backgrounds of gardens and homes and the style of the photos themselves. Mostly, she loved the emotions. Here was naked affection between siblings on a beach, the water and sky faded by age while their love was still clear and vibrant. There was an earnest smile from a child to her photographer, her closed lips suggesting she was self-conscious of lost teeth.

Eden remembered that feeling and smiled with sympathy.

"Eden?"

"Oh, I know, I'm sorry. I couldn't resist. You look so much like your father and his brothers, don't you? And the girls all look like your aunt. This whole side of your family stamps everyone out like carbon copies. I don't know why I find that so endearing, but I do. Your sister takes after your mother, though. They're both so pretty."

Except— The strangest thing happened. A trick of light on the glass of the frame over a preadolescent snapshot triggered the most bizarre, random sense of... *I know that face.*

Eden had seen Yasmine's photo online with Remy. They were all pictures of her as an adult with her tall, curvy frame, her ultrachic clothing, her hair in locs and her femininity emphasized with bold eyeliner and thick lashes, and lip colors like blue and mauve. She was clearly artistic and effusive.

Yasmine had her mother's skin tone, too—lighter than Remy's and his father's. Lighter than her mother, actually. As Eden stared at a nine-or ten-year-old girl, she saw another, similarly aged face. One that was Caucasian, before he had grown facial hair and thick eyebrows and a hard jaw and an Adam's apple.

"Oh, my God." She backed into the opposite wall and leaned there, afraid she would faint again for an entirely different reason.

"Eden."

Remy's voice came from the other side of the universe, but it was so quiet, it might as well have been inside her own head. He knew what she was seeing. He knew that she knew and she knew that he knew.

She began to shake. "Does Micah know?"

Remy seemed to be holding himself under such pressure, she half expected him to split out of his own skin. His head jerked once in negation, but it was his only movement. The rest of him was held in paralytic stillness, the way one stood when facing a deadly viper looking for an excuse to strike.

"No one does," he rasped. "Yasmine doesn't."

Why not? Eden tried to say it, but the ugly truth hit her like a meteor—jagged and explosive. Devastating.

CHAPTER TEN

"EDEN DOESN'T FEEL WELL," Remy told his aunt. Neither did he.

Auntie Celeste was a medical doctor, but she was also a woman shrewd enough to glance between them and understand something emotionally catastrophic had occurred.

"Take her home to rest then," she murmured.

Remy did and, once there, followed her into the living room where she sank, zombie-like, onto the sofa. He was too restless to sit and felt her gaze follow him as he paced.

"How…?" Her voice strangled on the word.

Remy began to talk without making the conscious decision to do so.

"After my dustup with Micah, my parents were worried Gould would start harassing them again, impacting the lives they'd made in Canada. That's when my father told me the first part—the part I told you. He insisted they'd been robbed and told me not to get into any more shoving matches with Micah." *Stay as far from him as you can.*

"The next time we had a game with that school, Micah was gone. I mostly forgot about the whole thing. A few years went by, then Yasmine got sick. It turned out to be a blood disorder that she has since learned to manage, but at the time they thought it might be leukemia. By then I was closer to fourteen, capable of researching what a bone-marrow transplant was. I said I wanted to donate mine. My mother brushed me aside. It was…" He pinched the bridge of his nose, still hurt at how abruptly she had dismissed him.

Don't be foolish. You can't.

"It was trying times for them. Obviously. My mother wanted my sister to be well, but I overheard her arguing with my father. What if they had to ask *him*. What if he *took* her?"

"Oh." Eden breathed in a sense of discovery.

"Yes. That was their greatest fear, right from the beginning. I cornered my father and he completely broke down, terrified that he would have to go crawling to Kelvin Gould to save his daughter's life. Terrified that Gould would let Yasmine die, rather than help her, purely out of spite. He swore me to secrecy, of course. Then Yasmine came out of hospital and I carried that secret with him." *For* him. "I never even told my mother that I knew."

He rubbed the center of his chest where the weight of it felt heavy enough to crack his sternum.

"It wasn't an affair, was it?" Eden asked sadly. "Did your mother go to the police?"

"No. She didn't even tell my father right away. He was working in the Netherlands, finalizing that prestigious contract. He was on top of the world when he came home. She had recently been awarded a lucrative research grant. He could tell she wasn't herself, but she made excuses. She told him later that she was trying to pretend it hadn't happened. She couldn't keep pretending once she realized she was pregnant. She honestly didn't know if Gould or Dad was the father."

Eden released a sob of agony. "Can you imagine that decision?" she asked in a voice scraped thin with anguish. She pressed the heels of her hands into her eyes. "I'm so sorry, Remy. So sorry she went through that. That you all did."

"It's not all tragedy. Yasmine is a gift. We all love her. It's not her fault that—" He couldn't finish.

"I know," she murmured. "I can tell you love her with everything in you."

"I do." He rubbed his face, trying to work feeling into his numb skin. "But loving her doesn't mean my parents weren't angry. Mom couldn't stay where she might see Gould. She suggested the move to Canada and my father agreed, but it was too much for him to let Gould benefit from what he'd developed. He struck back the only way he could. The only way that mattered to Gould."

"Money," Eden said, guessing.

"Yes. He threw his laptop in the river and sent the backup files anonymously to the competitor."

She nodded slowly, taking in all of what he'd said while tangling her fingers in her lap. Her thick lashes lifted.

"But all of them are gone now. Why haven't you told her?"

"I can't." His voice grew unsteady just thinking it. "I don't care where the DNA came from that made her. She is my sister in all the ways that matter and I will protect her with every fiber of my being. Even from—*especially* from—information that could destroy her."

Eden started to say something, but thought better of it and swallowed it back.

"You took down her photo." She pointed at the wall. "You knew I would guess."

"I forgot about the ones at my aunt's house." Had he, though? Or was he so weary of carrying this heavy secret, he'd allowed her to discover it?

He went long periods without really thinking about it, but lately it had sat like a pearl in an oyster, growing bigger and more intrusive the more he tried to ignore it.

Because it stood between him and Eden?

This was why she was such a danger to him! He had not only broken his father's confidence, but he had also broken it with *her*.

"Remy." Her voice was very quiet. Very grave. "Micah needs to know."

"No." He swept his hand through the air with finality.

"He can't keep thinking your family is the one who wronged his."

"Have I just made the worst mistake of my life by trusting you?" he asked in his hardest voice.

"I won't tell him." She sat straighter. "But you know I'm right. This feud has to stop."

"No. He has to grow up and leave me alone. We all have to keep our distance." He pushed his hands through the air, feeling a pang in his chest as he included her.

"I disagree." She swallowed and sat even

taller as she seemed to gather her courage. "I think we should marry."

"What?" Remy's eyebrows crashed together.

Eden's heart flipped over. Her thoughts were tripping over each other, taking in crimes and astonishing outcomes, so much pain and blame and protectiveness and love. At the heart was an innocent woman who deserved to know her kin, even if she didn't know he was kin.

"We have to become a family. *She* has to become Micah's family."

"Yasmine doesn't need a family like his," Remy growled.

"Micah can't help the family he grew up in." Eden rose to pace off her agitation. "My mother did what she could, but he was his father's heir. He wasn't given a choice about stepping into his father's shoes and running an empire—"

"He had a choice," Remy interrupted scathingly. "We all have choices."

"Yes. I have the choice to walk away from my father's legacy, too." She waved a hand. "If I don't want to marry for money, I can sell off rural branches and doom small communities to driving out of town for their housewares. The choices we're faced with aren't always good ones."

"That is why you want to marry me." His pointed finger stabbed the air. "To save your company. Don't pretty it up."

His words went straight into her like a blade, but all she could think of was Micah and the emotional deprivation of his childhood. She and her mother had poured love all over him when they could, but it hadn't been enough. That's why he was such a hardened cynic. It broke Eden's heart that he had missed all those years with his other sister. That Yasmine had missed getting to know him. That she had been taught he was the enemy.

"I want to right the scale." Eden's voice cracked under the pressure of her emotions. "This feud has to stop. Micah and your sister deserve to know each other, even if they don't know they share genetics."

"They'll figure it out if they're sitting across the dinner table, won't they? Then she has to learn what his father did to our mother. No, Eden. It can't happen."

"Remy." She wanted to stamp her foot, but settled on rubbing her eyebrows with her thumb and fingertip, trying to find a delicate way to say this. "In the same way you believe your baby would have a right to your fortune, I know that Micah would feel Yasmine has a right to a share in his."

"She doesn't want a cent of that." His lip curled in disgust.

"That's not your decision to make, is it? She's an adult. You're treating her like a child."

"She doesn't need anything from him," he insisted. "She has a vibrant career and she already has a brother who will step in if she needs anything she can't get for herself."

"Careful. You're starting to sound jealous."

The dangerous flash in the grim bronze of his gaze chilled her blood, but she continued making her point.

"Micah knows his father was rotten to his core. He has made countless changes—at his own expense—to repair things and ensure the company is more ethical moving forward." Micah had returned ill-gotten art and donated questionably obtained properties to the indigenous people they'd been appropriated from. There had been an infamous "winter cull," when a number of executives had been fired for various harassment complaints and other corruptions. "By refusing any part of Kelvin's fortune, you're allowing him to continue avoiding the consequences of his actions, even after he's dead."

Remy bared his teeth in a snarl of dismay, rejecting a truth he didn't want to hear.

"Micah would want to do what he could to

right this wrong. He would want to compensate your family for your parents' lost careers and damaged reputations. I understand why you want to distance yourself. You want to protect your sister. I will respect that, but at least let me make reparations on his behalf."

"This has nothing—"

"Don't tell me it has nothing to do with me!" she cried. "If that history hadn't happened, you and I would have a very different relationship right now. Wouldn't we?" Her voice dropped to a more tentative pitch.

He looked away, not confirming or denying, which left her heart trembling in her chest.

"I'm in the middle of this cold war whether I like it or not," she said, pretending she hadn't needily asked him to tell her he wanted her. "Let me try to fix it."

"By letting me buy in to your company?" he snorted. "Gee, thanks."

"It will be to your advantage. I'll ensure it." She crossed her arms, trying to stem the ache emanating from the pit of her stomach at the risk she was taking. "You'll have enough control that you could annihilate my company. You can exact your final revenge, if that's what makes you happy. You can also ignore my situation and let my company go to hell and leave Micah to stand by helpless as it happens."

"I'm not like that," he growled.

"I know. I trust you. And Micah will be suspicious of whatever arrangement we come to, but this is my company and my decision. He'll have to accept it." She could already feel the weight of her brother's disapproval. Her mother's shock and concern. "At least there would be a cease-fire. Then, as you bring Bellamy back from the brink instead of ruining us, Micah will start to believe you don't have it in for him. If Yasmine were ever to find out, do you want to still be at odds with Micah? Or on civil terms?"

Remy made another animalist noise of discontent, turning away as he asked, "What would you get?"

You.

Was that her real motive? To spin out her time with him as long as she possibly could?

"I get to keep my company instead of watching it be stripped for parts." She hugged herself harder. "Our marriage doesn't have to be forever. It could be in name only and we could divorce in a year, if that's what you want. You would still have a stake in BH and G and Micah would still have to behave himself."

"And if you are pregnant, we'll marry, anyway."

She flashed him a startled look, heart swerving in her chest.

"You had to know that's what I would want, Eden." He turned to face her. "What was my alternative? Watch the mother of my baby lose her company? Live apart from my child? Hide them? No, I was putting off saying it out aloud because…" He grimaced and rolled his wrist to encompass all he'd just revealed.

Was that really all he felt for her? Possibly the mother of his child, but not…more?

His hands landed on his hips and he hissed out a sigh. "I don't expect you to sacrifice yourself for someone else's actions. Gould wasn't your father. It's not your debt to pay."

Sacrifice. She bit the tremble from her lips.

"Micah is my brother. I know you haven't seen his softer side, but he has one. He's angry with you because of me. If he ever learns he has another sister, well, good luck being the only pit bull in the yard."

Remy brushed that aside, not wanting to consider that scenario. Right now, he was more concerned with keeping the secret of his sister's paternity so she wouldn't be hurt.

Eden had a point, though. If Yasmine ever found out, it would be a softer blow if he and Micah had found some common ground first.

Or was that a rationalization so he could get what *he* really wanted?

"Would we...?" He searched her expression. "Continue trying for children?"

Her stomach sucked in and she swallowed. "If you want."

"It has to be something *you* want," he replied with such force she took a step back. "Consent is mandatory." He had just explained why.

"Sex and babies are two different things." Her lashes swept down to hide her eyes. "I assumed we would have sex. I wasn't sure about the babies." She hugged herself and cleared her throat. "But consent goes both ways, obviously."

Good God. He ran a hand down his face while his heart fishtailed in his chest.

This was madness. Madness.

If there hadn't been such an urgency to resolve her business problem, he wouldn't rush into it. They might have had a quiet affair until this lust had burned itself out. In a corner of his mind, he knew that marrying her would ignite multiple bushfires in both their families, not to mention impacting his friendship with Hunter. He knew his relationship with his sister could be changed forever.

All so he could openly bring Eden into his home and his bed.

"Are you prepared for the kind of pushback

we'll get?" he asked, fearful she wasn't clear-eyed to the repercussions.

"It's the right thing to do, even if we're the only ones who know it."

He wasn't strong enough to say no.

"Then we'll marry as soon as possible."

CHAPTER ELEVEN

REMY HAD SUCH a calm, unruffled persona, Eden had underestimated how fast he moved when he decided on something.

She supposed she had seen it before, when he invited her to that club after exchanging a handful of words. Also at the wedding, when he ordered her into his car without any waffling and when he had made love with her very spontaneously, then brought her to Martinique at the last second.

None of that made their decision to marry seem any less reckless than it was. At least with Hunter, she had a solid friendship with his sister and had dated Hunter long enough to get to know him a little.

Her relationship with Remy continued to be a headlong rush toward possible disaster. What if Micah had been right all along and Remy was out to destroy her while she was too infatuated to see it?

Knowing Micah would presume exactly that kept her from telling her brother what she was planning. Her mother would be equally alarmed, so she kept her in the dark, too.

The secrecy heightened her anxiety. It made her feel she was doing something wrong, but there was value in keeping her nuptials under wraps. Those investors who were rubbing their hands with greedy glee, expecting to oust her, would be ambushed by her announcement. She would throw the switch on their takeover before they had time to make any other dirty ploys. In fact, with her stock price down, Remy was buying up as much as came available, helping her cement their combined ownership.

As for the contracts, they modified the agreements she had negotiated with Hunter. Her groom would still own a huge chunk of BH&G, but unless she was incapacitated, Remy was obliged to support her leadership.

All of that should have reassured her, but Remy moved with such lightning speed and determination, she felt pounced upon. His decisions were made like a blade cutting through inconvenient obstructions, forcing a path toward his goal. Yes to this paragraph, no to that. Chop, sweep, get us *there*.

In the midst of her double-checking the legalese on the new contracts, he broke in with fresh information.

"Martinique has a month-long residency requirement. So does France. We can marry in Gibraltar within a day, so we'll tie the knot there after we attend my aunt and uncle's anniversary party. Where is your birth certificate? I'm chartering a flight for my assistant to meet us with my own documents."

"It's at my apartment." She blinked in bemusement. "Quinn might be there. She offered to take my suitcases to my apartment. I told her to stay there if she wants to."

Quinn usually spent her summers working in PEI, where rent costs were lower, but she had begun her doctorate and was looking for accommodation closer to the university.

She picked up the video chat right away. Her red hair was in a messy bun, her freckled face clean of makeup, and she was wearing a loose-fitting T-shirt with stars and moons on it. Eden's kitchen was behind her.

"Are you okay?" Quinn asked without even saying hello.

"Yes." Eden was taken aback by her urgent tone. "Why?"

"Because you were publicly thrown over two days ago! You're allowed to be an emotional wreck."

"Oh. Right." Eden spared a moment to take stock. Her veins were stinging with the stress of having a lot to do, her emotions were reeling over the news that Micah had another sister, but her mind was clear and her heart… Her heart felt stretched in every direction. "I'm not *great*. These last two days have been a lot." Understatement of the year. "But I'm doing well enough."

"Okay. I'm glad." Quinn didn't sound convinced. "Because I can come if you need me. Just say the word."

"Thank you. I—" Eden was genuinely touched. She loved her mother and brother with everything in her, but Quinn was like a sister. "I actually need your help. And I have to ask you to keep it a secret."

"I'll put it in the vault with the rest of them," she vowed promptly.

"You're the best." Eden curled her legs beneath her. "Can you go into my office? There's a key under the plant on the windowsill. It opens the middle drawer on the desk. I need my birth certificate."

Quinn was no dummy. She set down her mug and her expression became very grave.

"You know I'll do anything for you, Eden, but it's been *two days*. At least you got to know Hunter. Even at that, you didn't know enough."

"I know it sounds impulsive, but it's for the company." That was partially true, at least.

"Your dream was always to marry for love," Quinn reminded her. Pleaded almost. "That's why I was so hesitant about you marrying Hunter. You have always wanted what your mom had with your dad because your childhood was so much better than Micah's. Saving BH and G shouldn't come at the expense of your own wants and needs. You know that, right?"

"It won't," Eden insisted, even as her stomach clenched with fretfulness. "It's complicated, but can you please trust me when I say I'm in my right mind and doing what needs to be done?"

"I trust *you*."

"But Micah has poisoned you against trusting Remy." Eden sighed. "Was he awful when you got up to the hotel room in Niagara Falls?"

"He wasn't pleased." Quinn started down the hall.

"I'm sorry I jumped ship. Please tell me you enjoyed the room at least."

"Erm." Quinn plonked the phone onto the desktop so all Eden could see was the ceiling. Quinn's voice sounded higher, almost strained, but maybe she was simply pitching her tone so Eden could hear her as she moved to the window. "He did his yeti act, blamed me for being your best friend rather than his informant. I finished the wine and had a bath. Enjoyed the view."

"Good."

"Which is pretty much what I'm doing here. There's paparazzi downstairs. They know I know you and keep trying to come up. But, hey, Vienna lives in the building. You never told me that. We're having drinks later."

"I thought you knew. But their apartment is a convenience. They live in Calgary."

"Really? I must have misunderstood her. Okay, I found the certificate. What now?" Quinn came back on the screen to show it.

"Put it in an envelope, lock the drawer and—"

A noise at the door made Eden glance up. Her heart lurched when she saw Remy there. How long had he been listening?

"Would you like her there?" Remy asked quietly.

"Where?" Eden frowned.

His head tilt said, *You know.*

Their wedding? Eden swallowed and nodded jerkily. She wanted someone who loved her at her wedding, seeing as her groom didn't.

"There's room on the flight. Tell her my assistant will send her the details." He walked away.

Ridiculously moved, she blinked her hot eyes as she asked Quinn, "Would you like a free trip to Europe?"

"Always. But seriously, are you okay? Be real." Quinn frowned with concern.

"I am. I promise you, I am," she lied. "But I have to go. Remy's assistant will be in touch."

She ended the call, her chest tight with emotion. It was nothing for Remy to add a body to a flight and cover a few nights at a hotel. Such a small gesture shouldn't mean this much to her, but it did and she knew why.

Quinn was right. Eden *had* always wanted to marry for love. It was hitting her that she was. It was too soon, way too soon, to believe herself in love, but she was halfway there. Remy was considerate. He was protective and valued family. And the more she got to know him, the more she was convinced that he was *worthy* of her love.

Even so, she felt as though she was sliding down a well-greased slope, careening at an uncontrolled speed toward... The unknown. A broken heart maybe?

Remy still regarded her as an enemy of sorts. At best, they would be business partners with benefits.

Now would be the time to call a halt to this madness, but she wouldn't. Couldn't. She had

never been able to forget him, and marrying
him, being with him, felt bigger than necessary. It felt done. Whether they went through
the legal process of marrying or not, whether
she had his child or not, she was linked to him
forever. She was his and had been for a very
long time.

It made for more hot tears against her eyes.
They blurred the future she was sketching for
herself. What if she was making a horrible
mistake?

They flew overnight to Paris.

Eden was still feeling raw, aware that her attraction to Remy was far beyond fantasy and
infatuation. It was a very earnest yearning for
him to feel as she did. To want her in the same
all-encompassing ways she wanted him.

They shared a light meal, talking of inciden-
tals to do with the contracts and what sort of
gown she should procure for the party, but the
air crackled with discordant tension.

When they were finally left alone, Remy
said gravely, "I heard what Quinn said, about
your wanting to marry for love. Is that true?"

Eden wished she could make some quip
about love being a luxury she couldn't afford.
She wished she could downplay her dream as
a childish whim.

Instead, she asked unsteadily, "Isn't that what most people want? Don't you?" She tried to make the question a mild one, but her heart was tripping in her chest.

He took his time answering, voice heavy when he said, "Love makes you so damned vulnerable. I've never wanted more than liking and respect."

His words went into her like twin stilettos. How could he like and respect her when she was related to his enemy and needed his money?

This was exactly how she had felt after Paris, when she had put herself out there, been open and receptive and excited and suffused with attraction, only to be struck back with a hard knock from reality. Five years ago, Micah's words had made her feel callow and wrong to want so much from Remy. Today was the same, as she reckoned with his not having any real feelings for her. And he didn't want to have them.

Each of her breaths burned inside her lungs.

"I would argue that I am marrying for love," she said and heard his sharply indrawn breath. "Micah doesn't know that I'm doing this for him, but love isn't transactional. It's something you feel by giving, not getting."

As she sat in the truth of her words, some of her misgivings dissipated.

"I don't want to hurt you, Eden. Then I would be exactly what Micah is warning you against—someone who used his sister to get what he wants."

"What do you want?"

"You," he said with pained remorse.

A pang of agonized pleasure went through her.

"You already have me." She felt positively naked as she said it, barely able to meet his eyes, but she needed him to know this was about more than money and family secrets and potential babies. She needed it to be about *them*.

He held her gaze with facets of bronze and copper and gold all churning in his eyes.

She swallowed and had to look away, but as he rose, her heart swerved in her chest, swooping and dipping, then soaring as he held out his hand. She set her fingers on his palm and watched them disappear in the gentle crush of his grip.

He led her into the jet's sumptuous stateroom, where a pale bar of indirect light glowed above the bed. When he closed the door, the click of the lock sounded like the mechanism on a vault.

The way his gaze slid over her made every inch of her burn.

"I don't want to fall in love because even this…" He cupped her face. "This craving consumes me. I don't believe in witchcraft, but it's like a spell. I don't want to be helpless to it."

She dropped her gaze to his throat. His Adam's apple bobbed as he swallowed. Her mouth must have pouted with her disappointment because his thumb slid across her bottom lip.

"That wasn't blame. I'm trying to tell you to be careful. Don't see this as more than it is."

"You think I'm not cursed in the same way?" she asked with a trace of bitterness. She tilted back her head in time to see him flinch.

Then his mouth was on hers, his kiss long and thorough, not rough, but not gentle. There was a taste of regret when he drew back enough to look into her eyes.

"It feels like something bigger than I can control. That makes it destructive." His voice was quiet, but his words reverberated in her ears, leaving her trembling, but not in fear. In excitement.

Her hands rose to grip his wrists. "Destroy me, then."

Their next kiss was all the more powerful, imbued with the desperate longing that had gripped her ever since he had kissed her in a nightclub then glared at her with betrayal.

That anxious yearning had her pressing closer, fingers clenching into his shirt while her body flowered with need as she absorbed the warmth of his. She needed to take all of him into her. *All of him.*

He made a noise that seemed equally tormented and his arms hardened around her. He crushed her close and she reveled in that small ache of her bones and joints and flesh in the vise of his embrace. She gloried in the enormous hunger that drove him to do it.

They dropped their clothes away and it was all about contact. Touching and caressing, claiming and tasting and sighing at the sheer bliss of holding each other. They rolled back and forth as she splayed herself across him, legs interlaced with his, breasts loving the friction of hair on his chest. He pressed her beneath him and pinned her hips with the weight of his thigh, then teased her ear with his tongue and scraped his teeth against her throat. She pushed him onto his back and his hands skated down her waist and hips, claimed her backside and swept up for the weight of her breasts.

Wisps of doubt floated in her periphery, making her wonder if they would burn each other to cinders, but she brushed away the thought, letting the miasma of sensuality engulf her. In this moment, they had and were everything. She worshipped the heat of his neck and the hollow beneath his ear and the scorch of his hard shaft against her damp, aching sex. She gloried in the way his palms drew circles at her waist and hips and buttocks, while his mouth drank from hers again and again.

She loved his smell.

She loved him. She loved him so much.

A skeptical voice asked, *How?* But a stronger voice countered, *How could she not?* He had so many admirable qualities. Sexy and physically strong, but strong in character, too. Protective and principled and loyal. He was funny and capable of forgiveness, and he stilled to cup her face, forcing her to meet the banked lust in his gaze while he asked huskily, "Are you still with me?"

"Yes." She wanted to tell him she was falling so deeply in love, she would be with him forever, but she feared he would push her away. Her eyes were wet and she felt foolish for being so emotional, but… "I really want this. You."

She wanted to pour her love over him so she could wallow in the beauty of it.

She melted onto him and ran her lips across his chest and stomach, and lower, making him groan. His hand squeezed her shoulder, cupped her neck, caressed her cheek.

"No more," he finally said in a husky, tortured voice that thrilled her.

He dragged her upward until she straddled him again.

"Condoms are in the drawer," he said.

Their gazes locked. She wanted to say it wasn't necessary. She wanted to marry him and have his babies and grow old together.

She did as he asked and retrieved one, then tried to put it on him, only to hear him as he rasped, "Are you trying to destroy *me*?"

With a soft laugh, she let him take over rolling the condom onto his length, then rose to guide him into her, so deliciously satisfied when she was finally connected to him again. She splayed her hands on his chest and felt his heart beat against her palm. The strong, uneven rhythm traveled up her arm, made her own pulse skip, then filled her heart to overflowing.

This was love. It had to be because it was too perfect to be anything else. It was generosity and sharing and vulnerability. It was such incredible dedication to ensuring the other's pleasure, it could only be that beautiful, all-powerful force.

It held her in its tender, unbreakable grip as they began to move in flawless synchronicity.

Despite their exhaustive lovemaking, Remy didn't get much sleep.

He reached for Eden in the night, half-lost to a heart-stopping dream that she wasn't there. She slid close and murmured sweet nonsense. Moments later, they were immersed in passion and his dream was forgotten.

She woke him a few hours later, returning to bed chilled from a trip to the bathroom. Her cold foot found his shin and she ruefully apologized for waking him. Then her hand found his hardening flesh and she said, "Since you're awake…"

He couldn't seem to get enough of her.

Which worried him. It felt a lot like the way people hoarded necessities right before the supply was cut off. He felt as though he was storing up all the memories he could, from the explosive orgasms they gave each other to the sound of her breath when she was relaxed against his side, so he would have something when he had nothing.

They were marrying, though. She had said he already had her. Did she mean her heart?

He hoped not. He didn't want to hurt her, but he couldn't let himself fall for her. There would be an inevitable choice—her or his family. Such a split of loyalty would tear him apart.

He was already tense as hell at her meeting Yasmine at the anniversary party.

Perhaps Eden sensed it, or perhaps she was apprehensive as well. She was quiet through the day as she was fitted for a gown and went to bed early.

Remy made some calls, forewarning his aunt Hanameel whom he was bringing as his plus-one.

"You can't bring her here, Remy," she scolded. "After all that trouble she caused you and your cousin? She's one of *them*."

He drew a subtle breath of patience, understanding her concern, but he said, "Please don't judge her until you've had a chance to meet her, Auntie."

She *tsked* and acquiesced, but Eden was equally unsettled when her stylist arrived.

"Are you sure about this? I don't want to get between you and your family on your aunt and uncle's special day. If you'd rather leave me here…"

They were in a trendy apartment he owned in Paris, big enough for a bachelor who traveled frequently, but not ideal for a couple. Remy was already thinking about where they might look for something that would feel more like a home.

"I want them to meet you so it won't be such a shock when we marry. If they make you feel unwelcome, we'll leave."

"I don't want that!"

Neither did he. "We'll make it work. I promise. I have to run out for a few minutes, but I'll be back in time to change."

He went to a jeweler, where he bought her some earrings—diamond waterfalls in four columns that ended in a taper. He was thinking they would bring out the silver detailing in her gown, but he was unprepared for how well the gown would suit her.

She almost knocked him out of his tuxedo and into the wall.

Her hands fluttered against her strapless neckline and down the fitted silk against her hip. Long sleeves ran from her upper arms to her wrists, leaving her golden-brown skin naked across her shoulders and chest. A slit in one side of the skirt revealed her smooth thigh, her shapely calf. Lower, he took in her black suede sandals with silver heels. The hem of the gown was beaded with silver patterns that licked upward like flames.

"Is it okay?" She started to touch her hair, then thought better of it. She had released her natural curls so they were a bouncy, glossy halo with a side part.

"You're beautiful." He had to clear his throat. "I should have bought you a necklace, too." He opened the box and offered the earrings.

"You didn't have to— Oh." Her eyes widened. "I have these hoops." Her hand went to the thin gold he hadn't even noticed.

"Call it an engagement present."

"I still have to return the ring Hunter gave me," she murmured absently, seeming mesmerized by the earrings.

"Give it to me. I'll do it," he said in a surge of unmitigated possessiveness. "Will you wear these?"

"How could I not? They're stunning." Her look up at him was admonishing, but filled with helpless delight.

Minutes later, they were in the back of the car. He couldn't help angling to see his earrings glinting and sparkling through the shadowed interior, filling him with intense satisfaction that she had accepted them. That she wore his diamonds, not Hunter's.

Not that he was the sort of man who needed to put a stamp on "his" woman. He was genuinely relieved she wasn't in that marriage. She would have been deeply unhappy and he was sick with himself that he hadn't stopped it sooner.

Could he make her happy, though? He kept telling himself this was a business arrangement with a benefit of slaked lust, but what if his family rejected her? For Yasmine's sake, he wanted the hostility with Micah defused and hoped this marriage would do it, but walking into the actual party was a delicate dance on a minefield.

Eden was a naturally warm and gracious person, however. No matter how stiffly she was welcomed when he introduced her to different people, she smiled and showed genuine interest and soon charmed even his aunt Hanameel.

"She's easy to like, I'll grant you," she conceded when they had a moment on a balcony, where they were catching a breath of air. "But what is your endgame, Remy? An affair with her will only stir up her brother against us. Do you love her? Is that it?"

She sounded so disapproving, he quickly said, "No, of course not."

It felt like a lie. His heart lurched, but he said it again, more firmly.

"I don't love her, but I can help her in ways that will put our feud to bed once and for all. That has to happen, Auntie. It can't continue."

She searched his gaze and he had a sudden thought—*she knows*. His heart swerved again. She was his mother's sister and perhaps had been his mother's confidante, but he looked away, refusing to confirm his own knowledge. It was too painful to consider.

"Secrets are as heavy as grudges. You know that, don't you?" She squeezed his arm.

A sensation hit his throat, one that made it seem as though all the air had been sucked from his lungs.

"You're neglecting your date, Remy," Yasmine said, forcing them both to turn to the open doors, where Yasmine as standing with Eden. Yasmine was her colorful, effusive self, wearing a wildly radiant and flowing pantsuit. Her locs were draped loosely around her shoulders, her lips were painted gold. "I could see her from across the room, standing here waiting for you to ask her to dance."

Eden gave him a wan smile. "I didn't want to interrupt."

With his joints feeling rusty, he made his excuses to his aunt and invited Eden onto the dance floor. She was stiff in his arms.

"If you overheard—"

"I like your sis—"

They both stopped speaking. He nodded to invite her to speak first.

"I like Yasmine a lot. She's so bubbly and hearing how she talks about art… She sounds like a creative genius. Your cousin said that fashion might be her bread and butter, but she can make bread and butter look like a masterpiece."

Remy forced a smile of amusement. "I can't disagree."

"Yasmine said her propensity for being consumed by art contributed to her recent breakup. It sounds like it was serious." Her lashes lifted as she tilted a look of deep understanding at him. "I see why you'd hesitate to hurt her, especially now."

He nodded in curt acknowledgment. Her recent heartbreak did make him that little bit more protective. So did that disturbing exchange with his aunt. Yasmine was no more vulnerable than the average Black woman. In fact, she had an incredible safety net in their large, wealthy family, but he wouldn't want her to feel as though any of that didn't belong to her or had slipped beyond her reach.

"Do you want to…?" Her lips rolled inward. "Invite her to…?"

Their wedding? It was partially for Yasmine's sake.

"Maybe."

One of his uncles cut in on him, eager to

tell Eden about his award-winning roses. They didn't talk about it again until they were aboard the flight the next day.

"You decided against inviting Yasmine?" Eden asked cautiously when they were in the air.

Her heart was still stinging at overhearing him last night, when he had assured his aunt that he didn't love her.

"I didn't want to do it at the party. Too many people around. I texted her this morning, but she probably stayed late and was still asleep. I made arrangements for her to catch up with us if she wants to. There's time before the wedding tomorrow."

Technically, they could have married on arrival and stayed overnight to fulfill the residency requirement, but this way they had time to relax in their suite, make love then lazily rise and enjoy the setting.

Eden texted Quinn, inviting her to join them on their terrace for an aperitif, then stood at the rail to take in the view.

Across the placid sea, the muscled coastline of North Africa was silhouetted against the reds and golds of sunset. A light breeze rippled the caftan she was wearing. Her whole body felt like warm honey, her mood expansive and light.

Remy joined her, wearing only a pair of drawstring joggers that hung low across his hips. He braced his forearms on the rail and cocked one knee.

Eden nearly swallowed her tongue at how casually sexy he was. She set her hand on his shoulder and skated it across his sun-warmed back, purely because she could.

And because she liked hearing him catch his breath and feeling him twitch with pleasure under her touch.

"Where will we marry?" she asked, hearing her voice waver with the potent emotion taking her over.

"In the garden. There's a gazebo near a fountain. We're the eleven o'clock. They do this all the time." He turned his head. "Do you mind that it's small?"

"Gosh, no! As long as you show up, it will be the best day of my life." It was a lame joke at her own expense, but so true that she experienced a sharp ache in her chest. At the end of the day, that's all she would ever need. Him.

"I'll be there," he promised with a laconic smile. His eyelids grew heavy and he straightened to drew her into his arms.

He needed a shave, but she liked the scrape on her palm as she cupped his jaw.

Everything in this moment was so perfect—

the man who was soon to be her husband, the intimacy of this moment, the sureness inside her that this was meant to be—she couldn't stop the words from tumbling out of her.

"I love you."

He didn't move, but she felt the stillness that came over him. She saw the warm light fade from his expression.

"I...thought you should know." She felt as though she had stepped off this balcony and was now only held up by his strong arms—arms that were falling away from embracing her.

He licked his lips.

"I was hoping this could be a real marriage," she said hurriedly. "One where we plan to stay together all our lives, not just for now. One that's about *us*—"

"Eden, *stop*. You know I can't think like that. For God's sake, we barely know each other. This chemistry..." He waved between them. "That's all this is. You have to know that."

His words were such a blow, she stepped back and tried to swallow past the jagged ache in her throat.

"This *chemistry* has lasted five years. For me, at least," she added weakly. She turned her hot eyes to the horizon. "I wasn't asking for you to say you love me, only that maybe you could. That you *wanted* me forever."

"How can I say that when wanting you goes against what's best for my family? I've let myself be carried along by this...madness." He flicked his hand through the air. "It's selfishness on my part. I'm trying to convince myself I can have you, have sex, without consequences. Now you're telling me it will impact you in ways that—" His profile winced with deep torture. "I don't want you to love me. Why did you have to say it?"

She didn't have a response for that angry accusation. She was so hurt, she wanted to hurt him back. She wanted to say, *Because I don't lie. Because I don't hide things from people just because it's hard for them to hear it.*

That wasn't love, though.

She stood there encased in pain, mouth quivering, trying not to cry. Trying not to make it worse, but what could she do? What would *they* do?

Into the charged silence, she heard a knock on the interior door.

She seized the excuse to walk away from him. Maybe in the back of her mind she thought it would be Micah, but she should have known it would be Quinn.

"Hi!" Quinn's bright smile dropped off her face. "What…?"

"Take me to your room? Please?"

"Of course. Let's go."

CHAPTER TWELVE

REMY CAUGHT THE brunt of Quinn's accusatory glare as she swept her arm around Eden, but Eden didn't look back.

The door closed with a heavy click, leaving him with a knotted stomach and a sick taste of bile in the back of his throat.

How could she believe she loved him? How? It was too soon. She had to know that.

Yet he felt as though he had broken her heart. His own was tangled in canes of thorns.

This chemistry has lasted five years. For me, at least.

He pinched the bridge of his nose. Had he led her on, telling her how longing for her had gripped him all these years? It was physical, though. Wasn't it?

The jangle of the room phone crashed into his tortured ruminations.

He snatched it up, thinking that if it was

Micah, he would gladly let the man kick his ass for hurting Eden.

"Remy?" It was Yasmine. "Can we talk?"

"You're here?" His heart nearly came out his throat. "Where? I'll come to you."

She told him and he quickly pulled on a shirt, trying to muster a semblance of clear thought at the same time. What should he tell her about asking her to come here? Was his marriage even still on?

Eden's need of financial help remained, but their marriage was also supposed to defuse the feud. It was supposed to bring Micah and Yasmine together without having to tell her the truth about her conception.

Everything in him balked at relaying that deeply painful truth to her, but his aunt's words came back to him. *Secrets are as heavy as grudges.*

He leaned against the wall of the elevator, nearly buckling under the weight of this one. Yasmine *was* an adult. Eden had gotten that right. He didn't want to tell his sister the truth, but he was starting to think he would have to. Not for any reason except that she deserved to know.

The doors opened and he moved with pained purpose down the hall, then rapped on her door and gathered himself for the difficult task as she opened it.

She was wearing torn jeans and a loose blue T-shirt. Her locs were gathered behind her neck with a yellow scarf and her face was clean of makeup. He might have dismissed her plain appearance as a slow start and a mild hangover, but her eyes were red and she seemed almost gray beneath her usually healthy glow.

"What's wrong?" he asked as she led him into the sitting area of her studio suite.

"Auntie Hanameel told me."

"Told you… What?" The words gusted out of him as though he'd been punched.

She nodded, seeming shell-shocked.

He did the only thing he could. He wrapped his arms around her and hugged her as hard as he could, feeling her trembling, but maybe that was him.

"I wanted to tell you myself. I didn't know how," he choked out.

She nodded jerkily, sniffing and holding on to him.

"It doesn't change a thing about who you are to me." He was clenching his eyes against a sting of tears. "You are my sister and I love you. Always."

She nodded.

"How are you doing with it?" He drew back a little, trying to see her face.

"Shocked," she mumbled and wiped at her wet cheeks. "Maybe not as shocked as I ought to be. I always thought there was something different about me."

"You're perfect. Okay? Believe that? Please?"

She nodded, blinking her wet lashes, mouth still unsteady as she sank into a chair.

He folded into the one opposite.

"Why…? I only realized last night that Auntie might know." His voice was a dry layer peeled off his heart. "Why did she think today was the day?" He ran his hands up and down his thighs, guilt a heavy mantle on him as he suspected his bringing Eden to that party had been her impetus.

"She asked me to come see her this morning. She wanted to know if I thought you were serious about Eden. I said I imagined so, since you had texted me to meet you two in Gibraltar."

"You told her that?" He bit back a curse of remorse.

"I was excited. She said it was time I understood what the animosity between you and Eden's brother was really about." Her voice was unsteady. "Remy… Does he know?"

"Micah? No."

"Does Eden?"

"She guessed. She—" He rubbed his brow. "It's complicated. We made it complicated. I was trying to protect you, trying to end this feud, and really…" He shook his head as he opened his eyes to reality. "I think we were just trying to find a way to rationalize marrying and being together when our relationship isn't rational. I don't want to hurt you, sis. I've been trying to find a way to make it okay that I'm involved with someone who is related to…" He searched her face, not wanting to say it aloud.

"The son of my biological father? It's not Eden's fault. It's not Micah's. I'm going to need some time to put all of this right in my head, but I know there will come a time when I want to meet him to…" She shrugged. "See if… I don't know, if we have things in common? It's weird. It's like I found out I was adopted. I have questions, but I also need time."

"Of course." He reached across to squeeze her hand. "It's enough that I don't have to hide it from *you* anymore. I won't say a word to anyone."

"And Eden?"

"She wants him to know, but she won't tell him. I'm sure of that," he added as he read Yasmine's skepticism. "She's…" Eden was *good*. She was kind. She was loyal and so heart-forward it scared him.

It made it really easy to stand right on her softest feelings and grind them to dust.

He hung his head in his hands. His elbows dug into his knees.

"Did Auntie send you here to stop us marrying?" he asked.

"She didn't know what to think of you two, but I pointed out how you had barely taken your eyes off Eden all night. That you're in love with her." It was a statement, not a question.

"I am," he admitted to her and himself, realizing only as his inner being shook under the impact that he'd been plunged fathoms-deep over his head. "It doesn't make sense because we barely know each other, but I think I fell for her the moment I saw her. I don't even believe in love at first sight."

"Because you're like Daddy, wired for mechanics logic. You have never believed in things you couldn't see and touch. You think planes fly because of physics, never wanting to admit physics is an incantation."

He ran his tongue over his teeth, letting her have that one because her teasing meant she was coming out of her tailspin.

He wasn't. It was hitting him that he had pushed Eden away for exactly the reason she had just said—he didn't understand how his

230 WEDDING NIGHT WITH THE WRONG BILLIONAIRE

love for her had happened, so he struggled to believe it was real.

"Is love magic?" he asked with a break in his voice. "Can I conjure it back if I've ruined things with the only woman who will ever make me happy?"

She wasn't pregnant.

Eden had thought her situation couldn't get any worse and, logically, she knew this simplified things, but when she came out of the bathroom, she was even more devastated than when she'd gone in.

The thought of having Remy's baby had been such a sweet one. Losing that possibility was a hard blow, one that felt very final. She was really freaking *sad*.

Quinn hugged her and tried to console her, but it didn't help.

"I thought he was The One," she told Quinn through her tears. "I thought we were soul mates. I know that sounds delusional."

"It's not," Quinn soothed. "Not for you."

"Because I'm immature? I wanted to believe destiny kept bringing us together. It was just coincidence and fixation. Lust. Micah always says that love is a lie people tell themselves to justify having sex. He's right."

"Your brother is a very cynical man. I'm

pretty cynical myself, but we both love you and your big-hearted optimism, don't we? It's not immaturity to see the world in a brighter light. It's necessary. Otherwise we'll all sink into bleak pessimism. If Remy is too blind to see what a gift you've offered him with your love, then he doesn't deserve you."

"He does, though! That's the worst of it. He's a good man, Quinn. He's honest and strong and caring. He loves his family so much, but he doesn't love *me*. He can't."

Quinn's brow furrowed. "Because of Micah?"

Eden took a breath, thinking...*kind of.* But that would open up more questions and she couldn't reveal the secret Remy carried about Yasmine.

Her breath left her in a sob of despair. She curled herself tighter into the sofa, feet on the cushion next to her, whole body leaned weakly into the back.

"Oh, sweetie." Quinn rubbed her shoulder. "We're going to take this one minute at a time, okay? I'll make some tea." She glanced to the kettle and coffee maker on the sideboard.

Eden wasn't thirsty. In this moment, she really didn't care if she evaporated from dehydration, but she could tell Quinn felt deeply helpless.

"Water is fine," she rasped.

Quinn nodded and rose, but halted when her phone rang. They shared a look, both aware it was likely Remy.

With a wince of persecution, Eden nodded that it was okay for her to answer.

"Hello? Yes, she's here." Quinn held the receiver to her breast. "He wants to know if you'll meet him in your room?"

Eden briefly dropped her brow onto her up-raised knees, but the one thing she had learned from her first wedding was that it was better to cancel it rather than hang on to whatever expectations she'd had for her future.

She nodded and forced her feet to the floor. "I don't have my card for the elevator."

"I'll take you up with mine. She'll be there in a minute," Quinn said and hung up, then said, "If you need to, pack your things and come back here. Or call me to help."

"I will. Thanks." She lifted empty hands as she realized she hadn't even put shoes on before she had fled.

With her mouth in a flat, sympathetic line, Quinn picked up her own key card and led Eden to the door.

Outside, they heard a woman speaking. "Call me when you can."

Then it sounded like Remy's unmistakable timbre. "I will. I love you."

Quinn's eyes goggled with outrage.

Eden was so shocked she could only watch in horror as Quinn flung open her door to see if it was really him.

It was. Remy was embracing—

"Excuse us," Quinn said stridently.

"It's okay!" Eden squeezed Quinn's arm, holding herself upright as shock and relief collided within her, making her feel punch-drunk. "She's his sister." What a farce!

The startled pair in the open door across the hall broke their hug to stare at them.

"Hi, Yasmine." Eden's smile was an act of bravery and a very poor one. Yasmine must have rushed to fly in for their wedding and now it was yet another disaster.

Eden wanted to hang her head and scurry into the swamp. If any of this wound up in the press, adding to her first humiliation... Oh, who was she kidding? The paparazzi were probably outside right now.

She couldn't even look at Remy as they started stiffly to the elevator. Inside, a freshly married couple in full wedding regalia were beaming and staring with adoration into each other's eyes.

Eden was downright sick by the time Remy opened their suite and they walked into the luxurious rooms. The space still wore the stamp of their messy occupancy—a tossed shirt here, a pair of discarded sandals there. The doors to the terrace were still open so the warm breeze wafted in with the hush of waves against the shore.

Night had fallen, though. The rooms were shadowed and everything felt dark and empty.

Remy flicked on a light. "Eden—"

"I'm not pregnant," she blurted.

"Oh." Remy straightened and squeezed the back of his neck. His voice became deeper. Heavier. "Are you okay?"

"I've had my period before. I'm pretty sure I'll survive it." She cringed, immediately regretting her snap. "What I'm saying is, we don't have to marry." She paced a few steps, but didn't know where to go. "I'll honor all the negotiations with the business. I still want Yasmine to have…" Her voice trailed into a pang as she felt completely adrift.

It struck her that she really didn't care what happened to her company. She and her mother would be fine. Not great. It would be a loss financially and a terrible blow to Eden's sense of confidence in her ability to run a company, but BH&G had been in trouble when she took it over. She hadn't caused the dire straits it was in. She was simply failing to rescue it.

"Yasmine knows," Remy said, voice not quite steady.

"What? How? I didn't say a thing," she insisted as she flung around.

"I know. It was my aunt. Which makes me feel like a coward for not being the one to tell her." He pinched the bridge of his nose. "But she knows now and that's a good thing."

"Is it? Is she okay?"

"She will be, I think. She's not ready to tell Micah."

Eden nodded and hugged herself. "I can help when she is ready. If she wants."

"Thanks." He nodded and licked his lips, searched her eyes.

There was a long awkward pause that asked, *Where do we go from here?*

"Once she's ready to tell him, he can make his own offers of reparation." Eden realized with a sick jolt. "You don't want to go through with this." Why would he? "I completely understand. Neither do I."

She swept her hand through the air, pacing again. Moving on because it was the only choice she had, but she was walking across the broken shards of her own heart, making every step an agony.

"I'm disappointed," Remy said. His hands were fists at his sides, his expression agonized.

In her? So was she! Hot tears rose to her eyes.

"I'm devastated that you're not pregnant," he continued, voice urgent. Unsteady. "It makes no more sense than any of this, but I wanted a baby with you." He pointed at her, then waved at the world around them. "I wanted all of this. The marriage, the future that lasts forever. I wanted to help you fix your father's company. Not for Yasmine, but for *you*. I want your love, Eden. I love you."

Cupid's arrow went straight into her heart. It rose to throb in her throat and she was blinking hard, trying to clear her vision. "But—"

"But I thought I shouldn't want it. That I had to protect my sister. I was protecting myself. Love for family isn't the same as what I feel for you. That love is not this crashing force that damn near knocked me down the minute I saw you. Do you know that when I walked away from you in the Louvre, I kicked myself for not getting your number? But then I stopped worrying about it because I knew that I'd see you again. I just *knew*. Make sense of that for me, will you?"

She bit her trembling lips and shrugged. She couldn't, but it had been the same for her. She just knew.

"When I asked my assistant to meet us here,

I had him go to my home in Montreal and get this." He strode to the safe in the bedroom closet.

She went to the door and saw him withdraw a velvet box. He opened it and offered it to her.

"These are my mother's rings. I wouldn't give these to a woman who isn't my forever, Eden. I knew that in here." He tapped the spot on his chest over his heart, then his temple. "I didn't know how to put that knowledge into what I knew up here."

"It has been fast," she murmured, still trying to see him through her blur of tears. Bemused ones now. Bordering on joyous. Great bubbles were expanding in her chest.

"It's been five years," he said helplessly. "Do you have any doubt that you'll feel the same in five more? In fifty?"

"No. I think you're the only man I'll ever love like this. After we're both gone, I'll look for you in heaven. Or in the next life and the next."

"What about here and now, though? Are you prepared to spend the rest of this life with me?" He came to where she was standing in the doorway and went down to one knee. "Will you marry me? Not for any reason except that we love each other?"

She cupped his jaw and lowered to sit across his thigh, never breaking eye contact as she did, even though her whole body was trembling and unsteady. "It would be my honor to marry you, Remy Sylvain."

With reverence, he tried the ring on her finger. It was a little big, so he moved it to her index finger, then said wryly, "We'll get it sized later."

"We'll make all the adjustments we have to." She looped her arms around his neck, so filled with love, she felt made of it. "The important part is that we'll do them together."

"We will," he said solemnly and gathered her closer, sealing their vow with a tender kiss.

Yasmine teased Eden that she would never forgive her for not letting her design her wedding gown, but she heartily approved of Eden's choice.

It was a small wedding, so Eden had picked a minimalist style while she'd been in Paris. It was the opposite of the confection she'd worn for her wedding to Hunter. The body-hugging slip dress with a cowl neckline was classic and elegant. Instead of a veil, Eden chose a modest crown of silk delphinium blossoms.

Yasmine wore a wide-legged pantsuit in a darker blue. Quinn put on an ice-blue dress, cheekily musing that she should have worn the bridesmaid dress already owned.

The pair had chatted while Eden and Remy were working out their differences.

"She came across to assure me he really loves you," Quinn told Eden. "Then we cracked a bottle of wine and talked about the sad state of our own love lives."

"Do you know how happy I am that my best friend has already bonded with my new sister-in-law?" Eden was brimming with happy tears and now had to dab a tissue beneath her eyes so she didn't ruin her makeup.

A few minutes before eleven, the women went down to the gazebo.

Eden had no fear of being left at the altar this time. Remy looked up from his watch and his love for her was like a wall of bright sunshine that fell hot and bright against her as she walked toward him.

Eden was vaguely aware of Remy's assistant and the officiant, but couldn't see anyone but her groom. He'd shaved and wore a simple gray suit with a vest shot with silver threads on royal blue silk. When he took her hand, her knees went weak.

"That's Mama's engagement ring," Yasmine breathed with awe.

"Do you mind?" Eden bit her lip.

"No. I just…" Yasmine blinked emotive tears and bit her wobbling lips. "It tells me how much you mean to him." She hugged Remy and Eden.

Impossibly, Eden's heart expanded even more. She could hardly breathe.

"Oh. Old, new." Quinn pointed at rings and gown. "Take this." Quinn worked off her bangle, one with blue sapphires that Eden had given her as a birthday gift years ago. "Borrowed and blue."

"Careful. I'm going to start thinking you're sentimental."

"Guilty. I want that back," Quinn said and they all laughed.

"Ready?" the officiant asked, waiting for nods before beginning to read from a small book. "Today we witness…"

This was really happening. With each word, everything between Eden and Remy changed. She placed her absolute trust in him. She gave him her future and herself, but he gave himself to her in the same way. The words—vows that they repeated very solemnly—were sincere, but also irrelevant. They were already one.

They were joined in ways that no force could put asunder.

In moments, she was startled to find herself placing a band on Remy's finger. He put his mother's on her and a fresh bubble of joyous laughter rose in her throat.

"You are married," the officiant declared simply. "Kiss, if you wish."

Remy's warm hand settled against the side of her neck. Eden tilted back her head and looked into his eyes. She felt such calmness and certainty, such rightness, she closed her eyes to savor it.

His mouth settled against hers. The kiss was chaste, but so deeply imbued with their love, fresh dampness gathered on her lashes. She loved him so deeply, the words formed on her lips as they clung to his.

Into their exquisitely perfect moment, a furious male voice cried, "Eden!"

"Oh, my God," Quinn gasped.

With a hot jab of adrenaline, Eden broke away from Remy and spun to see Micah striding up the flagstone path toward them.

"Oh, my God," she echoed. "I know you are not here to ruin my wedding." She moved to the rail of the gazebo. "No one in this world would be cruel enough to do that to a woman shortly after the last time it happened to her."

"Did you tell him?" Remy snapped at Quinn.

"That you were here? No." She looked and sounded as shocked as Eden was.

"No, she didn't." Micah sent a scowl of betrayal in Quinn's direction. "I figured it out all by myself when you two were all over the headlines after that party in Paris, but I couldn't find you the next day. Flight plans are public record and there's only one reason you would bring her here. It's not to see the Barbary macaques."

"Micah." Eden gripped the rail of the gazebo. "This has to stop."

"No, *this* has to stop." He pointed at the gazebo. "Have an affair if you have to, but leave it in the Bermuda Triangle. In fact, don't even do that. He's exploiting you when you're vulnerable, Eden. He's trying to get his mitts on your company. Come. We're leaving."

"No, he's not," Yasmine defended hotly. "They love each other."

Micah's gaze shifted to penetrate the shadows of the gazebo.

"We're married." Remy stepped up behind Eden. He squeezed bolstering strength into Eden's upper arms, feeling her tremble, but also used his bulk to shield his sister from Micah. "It's time for you and I to put down our swords and move on."

"When you're pulling stunts like this? Like. Hell."

Remy felt the jolt that went through Eden. Odious as he found the man, he didn't want to get between his wife and her brother. Or his sister and her other brother, for that matter.

"You *hypocrite*." Quinn suddenly threw herself forward to stand next to Eden. "Get off your high horse. You're upset about your sister getting married in secret? What about *your* secret?"

Micah's head went back. "Stop right there, Quinn. That has nothing to do with this."

"Micah and I have been having an affair. It's been on and off for ages," Quinn announced.

"What?" Eden breathed.

"Why are you doing this?" Micah's temper was condensing like a nuclear reactor getting ready to blow. "Why here? Now? Like this?"

"It was completely consensual," Quinn quickly assured everyone. "I'm not accusing him of anything more than *appalling* double standards. Your sister is allowed to marry whomever she wants. She can save her company however she wants. She can flush it all down the toilet if she wants to. You are not the boss of everyone just because you think you are!"

Micah stared so hard at Quinn, she should have incinerated on the spot.

"It's me you're angry with," Remy began.

"No. It's not." Micah gave one cold blink that dismissed Quinn. His expression became so ruthlessly implacable, Eden pressed backward into Remy. He closed his arms around her in reassurance.

"Are you coming with me or not?" Micah asked.

"We're married. I love him."

"You really believe that?" Micah choked on a humorless laugh. "You can all go to hell, then." He pivoted and stalked away.

"Micah!" Eden cried.

Eden had never felt such a tear of allegiance. She wanted to go after her brother to smooth things over, but when she glanced at Remy, she saw he was looking at Yasmine, who was wearing a look of teary shock.

Yasmine was staring at Quinn. Quinn was staring into the space where Micah had disappeared. She had such a devastated expression, Eden reached for her.

Quinn shook her off and pressed a pained smile onto her lips.

"I'm okay. I picked him because he would never hurt me." She flicked her gold-red hair over her shoulder. "It wasn't serious. We only kept it from you because you've always said you wanted me to marry him. I didn't want to give you false hopes. You know my feelings on marriage. For *me*. This is totally fine for you." She was forcing cheerfulness that was clearly false. *"Congratulations."* She hugged them both, short and hard. "But I'm going to take a beat…" She thumbed over her shoulder then hurried away.

"Quinn!" Eden started to go after her, but Yasmine touched her arm.

"I'll go. She did that for me. I told her." Yasmine shrugged helplessly. "We had some wine and she said she knew Micah. I didn't realize she *knew* him. You two just…be happy. Please?"

Eden let her go and looked in the other direction, but Micah was long gone.

"Regrets?" Remy asked.

She took a deep breath and sighed. "No." She slid her arm around his waist and leaned into him. "Just sorry that I've hurt him. That Quinn felt such a need to protect me that she's hurting now, too."

"We can go back to Paris," Remy suggested. "Or wherever he's headed."

"He'll need time to cool off. Let me call my mom. I want her to know that I'm genuinely happy and excited to start our life together." She was.

His smile kicked up at the corners, exactly the way that she adored most. "Me, too. We should probably talk about where that life will *be*, though."

"There's an idea," she said on a small chuckle.

They pressed their smiles together, then enjoyed a longer kiss before his assistant cleared his throat.

"The, uh, next couple will be here shortly, sir."

"Right," Remy said wryly, drawing back and taking her hand. "One pair of many. I'd say we aren't special, but we damned well are."

"Damned straight we are."

Laughing again, he scooped his arm behind her and they started down the path toward their future.

EPILOGUE

One month later...

EDEN STARTED TO enter the elevator at her Toronto apartment building, planning to race upstairs with her new purchase, but she came face-to-face with Vienna, Hunter's sister.

Vienna had on her running gear and removed her earbuds. "Oh, my God. Hi! I thought you moved to Montreal?"

Within seconds, they had ditched their plans so they could catch up over brunch. Vienna didn't even bother to change since they walked to a nearby café that catered to yoga moms and entrepreneurs.

"I am in Montreal now," Eden said once they were seated. "Remy has a gorgeous Victorian greystone on Avenue Laval."

She smiled every morning at the joy of waking next to him, but the sunlight that bounced off the gleaming gold of the maple floors didn't hurt, either. Light poured through the etched glass in the partition doors and a curved staircase led to a second floor, where the original four bedrooms had been converted into a master suite with its own lounge, a massive bathroom with an infrared sauna and a private balcony. The top floor held a den, two guest rooms, a rooftop patio and a hot tub.

"I've been working from home while we create some executive spaces at the BH and G building there. I'm only here to see Mama and finalize a few things here." Like replacing the problematic board members.

"Quinn said you had offered to let her stay in your place here this summer, but I haven't seen her. Of course, that was when she thought you would be moving in with Hunter. Has she gone back to PEI?"

"She's still in Europe." And not communicating much. She wasn't ghosting Eden as ruthlessly as Micah was, but every attempt to reach out was met with a mention of research that was keeping her very busy. "How is Hunter?" Eden asked cautiously. "Remy actually went to meet him today, but you probably knew that. Is everything okay with him and…everything?"

"He and Amelia are actually great together.

Peyton is a *doll*. I hope you're okay hearing that?"

"Relieved, actually. I feel like I should send her a thank you gift," Eden joked. "I wouldn't have been as happy with Hunter as I am with Remy. I hope you don't mind hearing that."

Vienna gave a little "hmm" of amusement, but looked into her latte.

"Are you okay?" Eden frowned with concern.

"Better than a year ago, but... Do you want to hear a secret?" She wrinkled her nose. "Neal and I have been separated since your engagement."

"Seriously? I had no idea. I'm so sorry."

"I'm not. It's..." She shook her head. "Complicated. It's simpler when I live here and he stays in Calgary," she said dryly, then her brow furrowed. "I haven't had the heart to tell Hunter, not when he was going through everything with Amelia and you and Remy. You know what the press will do to us. He doesn't need yet another scandal about his sister's marriage falling apart."

"I'm sure he'd understand. He's your brother. He'll want you to be happy."

"I know. It's just hard."

Eden knew. She had disappointed her

brother and didn't know how to fix it. Whether Micah would let go of his anger once he knew about Yasmine remained to be seen, but even though Yasmine was starting to talk about meeting Micah, Eden and Remy weren't rushing her.

Eden and Vienna walked back to their building, promising to catch up again very soon.

That was when Eden remembered what she had run out to buy hours ago. She quickly did the test and was beaming when Remy arrived home a short while later.

"How did it go?" she demanded. She was bursting with her own news, but she genuinely wanted to know how it had gone with his best friend. Former? Or forever?

"Good." Remy nodded, still seeming introspective. "I told him a little more about the history between my father and Micah's. Not everything, but I wanted him to understand better how you and I happened. That we would have happened five years ago if history hadn't been in our way."

"I saw Vienna. She said he seems happy with Amelia."

"He said as much. In fact, I've never known him to be so enthusiastic about anything. He was acting as though becoming a father is akin to landing a man on the moon. He's only been one for five minutes."

"I'm sure you won't be like that at all," she teased.

"I don't need to become a father to tell people how happy I am. I have you." He drew her into his arms and gently squeezed her. "Whether we make a baby or make our family another way, that will all be icing. I have everything I want or need right here." He kissed her nose.

"Shall I put that to the test?"

"How?" He frowned down at her.

"Well…" She walked her fingers up the front of his shirt. "That thing we've been trying so diligently to accomplish looks like it may have happened."

"You're pregnant?" The words sounded as if they'd been punched out of him. His arms tightened around her and the biggest smile widened across his face. "Okay, I lied." He hugged her and she could feel him shaking. "I'm going to be exactly like that."

She laughed and twined her arms around his neck. When he picked her up, she fastened her legs around his waist.

He started to the bedroom, but stopped. "Can we…?"

"We definitely can."

"This life of ours just keeps getting better and better." Laughing, he carried her to the bedroom.

* * * * *

If you fell head over heels for
Wedding Night with the Wrong Billionaire,
check out the first book in the
Four Weddings and a Baby miniseries,
Cinderella's Secret Baby!

And look out for the next installments,
coming soon.

Meanwhile, why not explore more from
Dani Collins?

Married for One Reason Only
Manhattan's Most Scandalous Reunion
One Snowbound New Year's Night
Cinderella for the Miami Playboy
Innocent in Her Enemy's Bed

Available now!